Encounter

Science Fiction Short Stories & Novella

2nd Edition

A. K. Frailey

ISBN Paperback 979-8-9874047-1-3

Website https://akfrailey.com/

Amazon Author Page
https://www.amazon.com/A.-K.-Frailey/e/B006WQTQCE

Cover by James Hrkach and AK Frailey

A. K. Frailey Books

THE WRITINGS OF A. K. FRAILEY

Books for the Mind and Spirit

https://akfrailey.com/

Contemporary Literary Fiction
OLDTOWN Fly, Sparrow, Fly
OLDTOWN Brothers Born

Historical Science Fiction Novels
OldEarth ARAM Encounter
OldEarth Ishtar Encounter
OldEarth Neb Encounter
OldEarth Georgios Encounter
OldEarth Melchior Encounter

Science Fiction Novels
Homestead
Last of Her Kind
Newearth Justine Awakens
Newearth A Hero's Crime
Newearth Progeny
Newearth Relevance

Short Stories
It Might Have Been—And Other Short Stories 2nd Edition
One Day at a Time and Other Stories
Encounter Science Fiction Short Stories & Novella 2nd Edition

Inspirational Non-Fiction

My Road Goes Ever On—Spiritual Being, Human Journey 2nd Edition
My Road Goes Ever On—A Timeless Journey
The Road Goes Ever On—A Christian Journey Through The Lord of the Rings

Children's Book

The Adventures of Tally-Ho
Wise Home
Wise Home on Lily Pad Pond

Poetry

Hope's Embrace & Other Poems 2nd Edition

Contents

Introduction

My plan has always been to put my best work forward. Over time, I have reviewed stories and reflections I included on my website and corrected, updated, or even deleted some of the work. Imagine my surprise to discover that some of the stories I thought were simply "experimental," were actually liked by readers for their own merit. That made me rethink my objective.

Writing is a process, and characters—just like their stories—develop best over time. I have found it fascinating to read early work by an author for no other reason than to comprehend the long-term development that went into a particular scene or the sequence of events in a story. It is also fun to glimpse the background lives of characters—where they came from logistically as well as emotionally.

In this second edition, I have included not only the original publication dates, but I also kept the range of very early science fiction character stories all the way into character stories I am still developing for my next novel.

In my imaginary world, there is always room for more development. May the same be said of me as a writer.

Rain from a Cloudless Sky

Originally published on The Writings of A. K. Frailey
7/29/2016

—OldEarth—

Breathe. In...out.

Savor the sensation.

Oh, God, how do humans stand it? So many sensations all at once. The warm sun on the face, the chill breeze as it rolls over the skin, the sound of laughter, the scent of... What is that? Fried chicken? Yes, that's what Father called it. Fried chicken. Hmmm.

I wish Father hadn't left. I know what he thinks; I depend on him too much. But being here alone... It's strange. Humanity is strange. Heck, the whole dang planet is strange.

Better get used to it. Life's profession and all.

Breathe.

Okay, Jacob, you can't see me, but I'm watching you. I'm a Luxonian Guardian now, and I'm going to stick to you like... glue? Humans come up with the oddest expressions!

Uh, ho. No... You're not supposed to be doing that...

~~~

"Ma?"

"Jacob?"

"I'm here, Ma. I just wanted to see you."

"Oh, Jacob. You're not supposed to. Go on. I'll be all right. Go home…"

"You're not all right. You're sick. I want to help."

Silence.

"No one can help me now, honey. I can't lie to a smart boy like you. You gotta accept. Go home."

"Not without you… without Pa… Janie…"

"Don't! I wish I could… God, the pain—"

"Ma!"

Shuffling feet. A clucking tongue…

"Hmmm, huh! Come on, boy. Your mother needs rest. Let her go. You'll do her no good here."

"But, Ma!"

~~~

Breathe.

I can feel tears aching to free themselves from behind my eyes. God, how do they stand it? I suffered when my mother passed, but it was different. Our suffering is different. Too many sensations here. My head aches, my stomach's churning with bile, I feel shivery…

Yeah, Father… I remember what you said. Light beings are different. It's not so painful for us. I have to relax, accept. Their suffering informs them. It's part of them.

Breathe. In. Out.

Father, I wish you'd stayed.

Uh oh…. Jacob? What're you doing now? A letter? Well, that's good…I hope.

~~~

Dear Uncle Matthew,

I appreciate your offer, but I realize now—it'd be wrong. I can't help you. First baby Jane, then Pa, and now Ma. I can't do this. The trip west was supposed to give us a new chance...but now... I'm alone. I don't care anymore. California might be everything you say, but it doesn't matter...not to me.

Someone could've helped us. But no one did. Only one old lady gave Ma a place to die. And afterward, she told me to find my own place. She has troubles enough.

Life's too hard—

Jacob

~~~

Sniffling. A sharp click.

"Jacob?"

A chair falls over. Scurrying footsteps.

"Who the—? Where'd you come from? The door was locked!"

"Stop, Jacob. I know you can't understand but don't do it. It's not over. *You're* not over. You're only fifteen—"

"Don't move. I'll shoot, swear to God I will."

"If you shoot, I'll just return later. Listen, Jacob, my name's Cerulean. I'm from another world... I can't explain, but I've been sent here to...how do I say...to watch over you..."

"An angel?"

Thud.

"Get off your knees, Jacob. No, not an angel. A being—not so different from you. I'm from Lux, another planet. But, listen— Here, sit down. Are you going to faint?"

"No. Maybe...."

"Breathe. Take a deep breath. It always helps me."

"Yeah...I feel a little better. So, you're—"

"A friend. Now, put that gun away. Better yet. Let me have it."

"What'll you do with it?"

"That old lady who helped you—she's been robbed three times this year; she might appreciate it."

"You'll give it to her?"

"She'll find it. I'll make sure of that."

"And me?"

"California isn't so bad. You're a smart boy. Your uncle has a shop you might like. He's a doctor of sorts. You'd learn a lot."

"It won't make any difference."

"Listen, Jacob, if you stay alive...*you'll* make a difference. You'll save someone's life, many lives."

"How do you know?"

"I don't...not unless you're willing to try."

~~~

"You did well, Cerulean. Don't be afraid, you did the right thing. The Supreme Council has absolved you from your interference, but you know, there will be consequences...down the road."

"But wasn't it worth it?"

"Certainly. Part of being a Guardian involves risk. Personally, I find humanity worth a great deal of risk. They're surprising...the way they think...the way they love."

"They're not so different from us, are they?"

"No. But beware."

"What?"

"They're unpredictable. Like rain from a cloudless sky. Remember to breathe. In...out...."

Mirror Image

Originally published on The Writings of A. K. Frailey
8/12/2016

—OldEarth—

Viridian: Luxonian Light Being from planet Lux in training for Guardianship position on Earth.

Roux: Luxonian Guardian assisting Viridian.

Cerulean: Viridian's Luxonian father.

Viridian's Personal Report — Location: Los Angeles, USA, Earth

Training Day: 91

Another scorching, humid day amid a crowd of humans. This time I'm at some kind of Improvement Park. Pathetic. Cerulean told me I'd meet Roux here, and though everyone looks better than the ridiculous specimens I saw in the midwest, these versions of humanity look like they have intelligence factors of trog—
"Viridian?"
"Uh, yeah?" *Here we go. Some muscled troll looking for a fool to make his—*
"Hi. I'm Roux. Your father's friend."
"Roux? You're a Guardian?" *Okay, I'm at a loss here. This guy looks good. Dark skin, rippling muscles, and clear eyes—no one's going to throw bio-matter at him. When guardians copy*

humanity's best, they do have certain...advantages. Pity so few humans are ever at their best.

"Yeah. Something wrong?"

"No. Just, you look different. So healthy and..."

"Strong? Come on."

What's he chuckling about?

"Cerulean sent you over to try a new setting. This is a training center for Olympic athletes. You've got to be in good shape to fit in."

Sweat is still trickling down my back, but suddenly, I don't care. "Good. I'm sick of being a fat boy with bad acne. Being a human is worse than being in a Luxonian prison."

"Hey, stop. Your father probably wanted you to tough it out so you'd understand humanity better."

Here we go... "I understand. Trust me. I've been waddling around in this horrible shell for three months. I've been picked on, kicked, and treated like a scurvy animal. Tough-It-Out has been my middle name."

"Uh, huh."

Hmmm... Roux just turned around and started walking toward a large steel encased box, otherwise known as state-of-the-art human architecture. One of these millenniums, humanity might realize that nature has a head start on both beauty and utility. Better hustle. In this heat, I'll soon be nothing but a pile of calcified bones and a pool of sweat...

Yes! Air conditioning!

"Okay, Viridian, your job is to observe without being noticed. You'll keep taking notes... You have been taking notes?"

"Every moment."

"Good. You can edit later. But it's a good idea to keep a running log when you first start. Later, you'll know how to discern the important material from useless data."

"Yes. Certainly." *I'm nodding my head like a stupid puppy. There'll come a day—*

"So, how do you want to look?"

I have a choice? "Strong, like you." *Big grin. He likes that. So human.*

"Let's go over here; this room isn't being used. I have a key. We'll be able to work in privacy for a bit."

Okay, this is nice... I guess. Cresta torture chambers could do advanced studies here. The floor space is covered with every sort of exercise equipment humans can conceive of to get their flabby, skin-encased sausages into some sort of shape. And mirrors. Why? So they can see the sweat pour off their appendages like rain off gutters?

"Come here, Viridian. Stand in front of this mirror. Think about what you want. Make yourself take that form."

"Anything?"

"Anything human."

Bloody hell. "Okay, I want to be tall, bronzed, muscled...blue-eyed..."

"Think of some kind of ethnicity you admire and copy it.

Admire? That's a joke, right? "How about a Norseman?"

"You're a few centuries too late, but work on it, adapt it...make it fit the current setting."

Okay. Now... I like what I see. Tall, muscled, tanned, green eyes—

"Wait. You want to look good but not call attention to yourself. We don't want women falling over themselves to meet you."

"Let 'em fall."

Uh, oh. He's got Cerulean's "adult look" trying to stare me down, something the Guardians must have passed on from time immemorial.

"I need to make something clear here, Viridian."

Here we go again... Time to open wide my I'll-be-a-good-puppy eyes.

"Take a good look in that mirror. See that man. That man is you, the image that you're presenting to an entire race of beings. You and I know what you're really made of, but only you decide how to present yourself and what this body stands for on the inside."

Now I look sober and thoughtful for a couple seconds. "Yeah... I think I understand. Thanks, Roux."

Big smile. For such an experienced Luxonian Guardian, he's got the brilliance of clay.

"We'd better go. I've been following an athlete trying out for—"

I couldn't care less. I'm walking toward the door a new man...or a new man-image. All I've got to do is survive a few more months here. Humanity is heading for a fall—And I'm not going with them.

"—so, you understand?"

"Perfectly. Thanks again, Roux."

"Great. You go out first; I'll come right behind you. Just look natural, like you belong."

~~~

Roux's Note 374,653: *Cerulean, we've got trouble.*

The Human Question

Originally published on The Writings of A. K. Frailey
8/26/2016

—Planet Lux—

Capital City Qui

Assembly Hall: A stadium-sized room with a glass ceiling and a smooth stone floor, with multi-colored floras growing up the walls.

Luxonian: Light beings from the planet Lux who send Guardians out to observe alien cultures in order to protect their interests in the region.

Cresta: A techno-organic race from the planet Crestar with long, soft bodies, tentacles, and large, watery eyes. They speak in a synthesized voice, and their large brain sack lays hidden behind a spiral shell. They wear breathing helms when not on their own water-based planet.

Ingot: A cyborg race that wears bulky techno-organic armor and breather helms built directly into their bodies, from the planet Ingilium.

A tall, white-clad figure emanating a silver glow sweeps before an assembly of various interplanetary beings. He perches on a floating dais and rises through the air to the center of the room. His sharp, clear voice rings across the hall.

"Good day, fellow Supreme Judges, Minor Judges, Guardians, Civilians, and Off-Worlders. As the designated spokesperson for our Luxonian Coalition of Supreme Judges, I would like to introduce myself—in case there is anyone here who might not know of me—"

The assembly breaks into an assortment of chuckles. One Cresta actually snorts water over the top of his breather helm.

"My name is Sterling, and I've made enough off-world trips to understand the plight of an Exo who hasn't had a chance to catch up on the latest 'who's who' in the planetary system. You have my sympathies."

More chuckles. A kindly Cresta attempts to reassemble the snorting Cresta's damaged breathing helm.

An Ingot shushes them with a hiss.

"As you know, we are assembled here today to discuss 'The Human Question.' We have been watching humanity's activities for millenniums; in fact, Luxonians have led the way in new observation techniques through our Guardian Program. As humanity faces possible extinction, it is important that *we* decide our role in their future."

The Crestas in the assembly nod agreeably while the Ingots maintain stoic neutrality.

"The question before us is this: Is humanity worth the risk? At this point, they do not play any significant role in universal events. They have never taken part in any inter-planetary wars or treaties since they are unable to perceive their larger universal society. So, why save them?

"If you have an opinion, I would be glad to hear it. I will be available during the post-conference gathering for conversation and discussion. Please, feel free to partake of the viands provided and make yourselves comfortable. Debate the issue, consider it from all angles, and I will be at your service if you have any questions or thoughts on the subject.

"Thank you."

Judge Sterling lowers himself to the ground floor and steps off the dais. He smiles and waves as he enters the mingling throng.

Bureaucrats! As if I cared what they think. Still... one must maintain one's position in the larger arena. As long as they think I give a—

"Judge Sterling?"

Sterling whips around to face a hunch-shouldered Cresta dressed in a cumbersome mechanical exoskeleton.

"Yes, how can I help you...?"

"Taugron, from the planet Crestar. I'm a scientist—"

I have to smile, but I hold back the sarcasm. "Aren't you all?"

"Well, yes, rather. But I fear we miss the bigger picture when we only take the scientific angle."

A Cresta rebel? How...unique! I might find this little fellow useful.... "Please explain; I'm fascinated by your position."

"Ah, well, I must admit...I hardly ever get this far in a conversation. Most of my compatriots swim away at this point. But, I know you're busy, so I'll just say this: why can't we learn from humanity so that we can better utilize their strengths?"

14

"That's been the point all along."

"Yes, of course, but we, I mean most races, tend to look at humans as a sort of field to harvest. Couldn't we view them as possible allies—"

"Their obvious inferiority makes that unlikely."

"Not if we interbred—"

My colors just dimmed, perceptibly. I'm feeling ill. If it wouldn't be impolite to scorch this dwarfish Cresta into charcoal, without staining the floor, of course, I'd be glad to...

Taugron shuffles his three-toed boots and wraps his tentacles behind his back. "I'm sorry. I see I've offended you."

Cresta sludge... "Not at all. But I am being called. Please, excuse me."

Ah, here's my old friend and ally. What's her name again?

A six-foot Ingot female dressed in bright red, techno-organic armor sidles forward.

"Sterling! Lang. You remember me. From Universal Reports."

"Ah, yes, of course. My favorite Ingot this side of the Oskilth Zone. How are you? Keeping everyone confused, are we?"

"Lies and more lies. You know my by-line."

I would love this gorgeous cheat if she weren't such a bulky cyborg. "How can I help you, dear?"

"I want to shed some light on this human issue-thing."

"I'm waiting with bated breath." *Oh, why did I say that...she's clumping into my light space.*

"Humans are nothing. Let 'em die—naturally—of course. It won't take long. The Crestas would love to see it done a little quicker, but we're not going to get involved. What matters is—that planet of theirs. It's ripe for harvest. When the playing field is more level, remember your friends, all right?"

"Why should Lux have any say in the matter?"

"Don't play the fool with me. I travel everywhere and see everything. I know Luxonian interests. Humans aren't the only ones facing extinction."

Ugly Troll. Where did she— "I must say; you have an interesting assessment of the situation. I will keep it in mind."

"Do that. And don't forget my name—Lang."

"You'll be uppermost in my thoughts. Excuse me, I see a Guardian I must speak with...."

Uppermost in my nightmares, more likely. "Cerulean! Stop. I'll speak with you."

Cerulean, dressed in his usual human style with jeans and a collared shirt, turns from the assembly and focuses his sky-blue gaze on his superior.

"Yes, sir?"

"Next time you return to Newearth, I'll arrange a formal visit. We can discuss your position..."

"Certainly, sir."

"You don't look particularly happy."

"Happiness has nothing to do with it."

"What's wrong then?"

"It's just the way you discussed matters here, sir."

"Why? I have done everything according to protocol. I assembled all the leading citizens of relevant planetary systems. They are the ones who will be most affected by humanity's fate. Have I left someone out?"

"Yes, I'm afraid you have."

"Enlighten me."

"Humanity."

"Their opinion hardly matters."

"I disagree. In fact, their fate might mean the world to us."

"Why is that?"

"Because it will likely to be tied to ours."

"You will be returning to Newearth soon?"

"Yes, sir."

"Good. Remember where your first loyalty lies. Good-bye, Cerulean."

I shouldn't be so surprised. Ask a stupid question... Get stupid answers.

Horizon Line
Originally published on The Writings of A. K. Frailey
9/9/2016

—Human Remnant on Lux—

Year 34 After OldEarth

Ooohh, feeling kinda ancient today... If I close my eyes, I can almost smell oranges, honeysuckle, and Kendra's perfume...

"Hey, Doctor Mike."

I have to block the glare from my eyes to see the silhouette of a young man standing before me.

"Hmmm? Peter?"

"Thought I might find you out here."

"Step into the shade; I can hardly see you. Sun's so blasted bright."

"You're not wearing your sunshields."

"I'm sorta old for those things. Feel like a kid trying to look cool."

"May I sit?"

I glance at the cave-like hollow I have nestled from the sweeping branches of the mammoth tree and grin.

"Sure, the shade's for everyone. You know, this tree is nearly twenty thousand years old."

"Pretty impressive."

"About the only thing around here that makes me feel young, except every dang Luxonian alive."

"That why you like this spot?"

"Yeah, and the fact that few people like to hang out under the Luxonian sun, except Luxonians, and they don't usually sit on the ground under a spreading Niomi Tree."

He's shifting around, eyes darting. He's got something to say but….

"What's on your mind, Peter? You didn't come all the way out here to spend time with an old man—"

"You're not the only one getting old!"

Uh oh, his face just contorted into bitter ridges of rage, not something I'd expect from his usual cool, collected personality.

"Okay, let it out. What's going on?"

"Nothing. That's the problem. Mom and Dad always hoped I'd make it back to Earth someday but that's not—"

"Resettlement will happen. Just give it time."

He's on his feet again. Hmm, I didn't think there was room to pace like a raging bull in here. Guess I was wrong.

"Time has passed! We've been stuck on this planet for almost forty years. How long is it going to take before the Luxonian Judges deem us fit to return?"

"You've got to remember; a lot went wrong at the end. The entire Luxonian population carries vivid, grievous memories of those days. They don't want the whole cycle start over again."

"Who are they to decide my fate? I belong on my native planet. It's my right!"

"Slow down, boy. Listen to me; Mark and Jackie were two of the greatest human beings I ever knew, but they also had a blind spot when it came to humanity. They refused to see our dark side."

Now he's staring at me like I'm a traitor. Can't be helped.

19

"Like Luxonians don't have a dark side!"

"We all do. But we don't like to face it. You know all the old stories, but I rarely talked about my old friend and colleague, Doctor Peterson."

"You mentioned him."

"Yeah, but I never mentioned that he fell into madness before the end."

Flinging his body to the ground, poor guy's covering his eyes with his hands. He is so human. Refreshing after so many years of perfect Luxonian self-control.

"You're not helping. I want to get back. It's...I don't know, a calling, a need."

"You will. I firmly believe that. I wish I could go with you...but that's not gonna happen."

"You could—"

"Heck, Peter, I'm seventy...something. Luxonian years mess with my timeline. My life has been full to the brim, and I'm not complaining, but I know when my horizon line is drawing close. I won't live to see Newearth. But you will."

"When?"

"When the time is right. Now stop grumbling and help an old man to his feet. I've got something to show you."

Groan. Maybe I'm closer to eighty....

"Where're we going?"

"I've got a surprise. Cerulean's been helping me."

"What?"

"Boy, don't you know the meaning of the word—surprise?"

~~~

We just entered my inner sanctum. Okay, it's my hobby room. I stride (hobble?) over to my worktable strewn with various plans, stand tall (let an old man dream) and spread my arms wide.

"Now, listen. When I pass on, I want you to unveil this on the day they lay me in the ground. On Newearth."

I wave the holographic image into the room. It's every bit as gorgeous as the idea I carried around in my head for so long.

"Surprised?"

Judging by the wide eyes, dropped jaw, and shaking hands, I guess my surprise had the desired effect.

"Doctor Mike! By the Eternal, when? How?"

"I told Cerulean some time back that I had an idea for the first settlement on Newearth. He was kind enough to humor me. I'm not a holographic specialist, but he has a few friends, and we worked on this model for a looong time.... It's been a labor of love."

"It's terrific! Everything looks perfect to scale. It's got hospitals, schools, a business district...even a hilltop— What's that?"

"It's idea, a sort of dream really, an Inter-Alien Alliance where humanity would have our Capitol and aliens could come and petition for representation on Earth."

"It kinda looks like a church."

"Well, it's supposed to represent something bigger than us...something nearly supernatural. You can hardly understand how sheltered humanity was from the greater universe. I suppose we still are. We'll never be done discovering how much we don't know."

"But—"

"It's not a place of worship, but a place to remember and act like beings with vision...beings who still have a lot to learn."

"I'm...I don't know what to say."

"Just say that you'll do as I ask. Bury me there, in Newearth soil, and unveil this plan. Cerulean's been working with the Supreme Judges and they're close...very close. In fact, I believe that your son will be born there."

"Huh! If I ever have a son. No woman will have me."

"That little Miss Violet has eyes for you."

"She has eyes for every male this side of the Luxonian Divide."

"Then there's that shy Rose...she's a sweet thing."

"She's not interested in—"

"Listen, Peter, you're going to have to do some of the heavy lifting here. I'm an old man; I can't do everything. Here's your first settlement. Name it whatever you wish, just bury me there and get yourself a wife so you can bring your son to the top of that hill and tell him about me... Okay?"

Tears course down my cheeks, but I don't care. I'm an old man. And old men do foolish things, dream visions and ask for the impossible...after all...our horizon line draws near.

Enemy Self

Originally published on The Writings of A. K. Frailey
9/23/2016

—Intergalactic Trading Ship *Bountiful*—

Justine's Private Internal Record

Captain: Lu Kimberling

Hired Protection—Androids: Justine Santana and Max Wheeler

Ship's Lounge, Captain Kimberling steps in.

"Hey, you two, one last stop at Ingilium, and you can look for other work. I'm going to take a breather on Helm. The Bhuaci are harmless, so I won't be needing your services for a while."

Oh, joy! Wheeler is going to give his opinion. Like the captain cares....

"Are you certain that's wise, sir? The Bhuaci may be harmless, but they are frequently attacked. The Telathot incursion nearly decimated—"

Brilliant. Get the highest paying ship's captain irritated while light years from the next hope of employment.

"Don't lecture me, Wheeler. I've stopped there often enough and found myself a secure place. Cresta's and Ingots could invade till the sun explodes, and they wouldn't nudge me a millimeter."

Know the meaning of the word vaporized? If Wheeler were human, he'd be bright red right now.

"As you say, sir."

"Sure, compliance always makes up for being a total idiot—"

"Listen, I'm going to sleep. The crew just changed shifts and we're in dead space, so it should be nice an' boring for a while."

"As you say, sir."

"By the time I need you again, Wheeler, learn a few new expressions, would you?"

"As you—"

"Ah, shut up."

Poor Captain Kimberling. He hasn't got one itsy, bitsy clue...

~ ~ ~

One hour later...

Wheeler may be huge, but he's as bulky as an Ingot and lumbers like a Cresta. His brown, steady eyes peer straight through the lounge bay window displaying our bright, red spectrum universe as it swirls amid black space. I'd like to paint that view. Someday.

What does Wheeler think about in that tectonic brain of his? Here goes nothing... I'll be subtle. Promise.

"You do that on purpose, don't you?"

"What?"

"Egg him on."

"Egg. Him. On. What is that supposed to mean? No, don't tell me. Another one of your human colloquialisms? You need to decide what you are, Cyborg."

"Like you?"

"I have an identity. I know my role and I—"

"Play the fool."

"Who's the fool? You're the one pretending to be human. 'Look at me, I have a moral code...' You were lucky to come out in one piece on Terra Seventeen."

"I am human. At least...genetically."

His grip is stronger than I anticipated. Good to know....

"Shall I rip your arm off and show you the technology that holds you together?"

Twist, turn and elbow to the midsection. Leg sweep under the knees. Pinch Wheeler by the soft spot at the base of his neck...

"Let me remind you that when they put me together, they included the DNA of a brilliant human mind. Not a Cresta—"

"I'm not Cresta!"

"Ingoti then."

"Damn you!"

Pity on the fool. Oops, didn't mean to shove that hard.

"That almost sounded human."

"DNA means nothing!"

There he goes again. He really ought to turn beet red just to clarify himself.

"So, you're human too? Genetically speaking?"

"I'm a cyborg. Humanity never claimed me. I never claimed them."

"But your cyborg family welcomed you with open arms, right?"

"Go to Bothmal!"

"Please—watch your language."

"Like anything could offend you."

"I have sensibilities."

"Just no sense. Being human—genetically speaking—won't protect you. Only a cyborg—"

"You won't live forever."

"Near enough. Better than anyone else."

"Uanyi and Ingots live for millenniums. Luxonians too. Are they happy?"

"Hades! Who's looking for happiness? I want to survive for as long as possible."

"Someday...you'll die."

"Not if I can keep getting parts. Besides, who really cares?"

"That's the question, isn't it? You've never given anyone a reason to care—"

Uh oh... blinking, blaring sirens! As usual, humans typically overstate the obvious. Here comes the captain, charging ahead like a Cresta at a science convention.

"Hey, you two, looks like we've got unexpected visitors. Power up!"

Sigh. Wheeler's got bloodlust in his eyes again.

"Ready, Human?"

"As much as you, Cyborg."

"Don't look so grim. We'll come out of this alive. Probably. It's a living."

I wonder...

"Or a really long death sentence."

Dedication

Originally published on The Writings of A. K. Frailey
10/7/2016

—Newearth—

Oh, Lord, why do human beings insist on performing these ceremonies? I bet Doc Mike himself wishes they'd get on with it and just bury his remains. The Governor is as wordy as a Cresta at an Inter-Alien convention.

"...and as Peter, son to two other magnificent examples of humanity's finest, so touchingly reminded us, Doctor Mike was the guiding light behind this new beginning. As Governor, and in effect, Commander in Chief of—"

Pul-leez, Commander in Chief, Raymond? Of a couple hundred kilometers? Tuck that ego in a bit.

"...we'll know prosperity and good fortune into an unimagined future here on Newearth, all starting from our humble beginning in—"

We'll all pause now for dramatic effect.

"...Mikestown."

Breathless silence. And I do mean, breathless. It's so hot and humid, why on Newearth did he pick July, of all months, to have this dedication ceremony?

Doctor Mike's remains descend slowly into a marble receptacle. An engraved slab slides over the top. Luxonians in full regalia steer a life-sized statue of Doctor Mike to the grave and center it on a marble stand.

The end! Please, make that the end. Oh, no, he's starting up again with a smile that knows no bounds.

"...And I would like to invite our newest citizens and Luxonian guests to our modest repast before we begin this new and challenging—"

"Thank you, Governor Ronald Raymond!"

A tall Luxonian woman, with three human attendants, gestures politely toward the assembly hall situated on the west side of the Capitol building.

Thank God! Saved by the cooking staff.

~~~

"Hey, Cerulean! So, what do you think?"

Peter's smile is always so genuine. He reminds me of Anne. I hope—No. Better not go there.

"Hello, Peter. Mission accomplished. You always said that you'd see this day—"

"No, actually, that's not true. I'd have given up but for ol' Doc. You want a sandwich or something?"

"Sure. The cook is a friend of mine. I'd better partake, or I'll have a lot of explaining to do."

Hmmm.... Where did they get chickens? Forget it. Peter looks happier than I've seen him in a long time. Must be a weight off his mind.

"So, where's Angelina and the baby?"

"They're helping with the food. Several of the attendants took sick after the resettlement, so she's been managing...sort of."

"Good of her."

"Not really. It's a dream come true, settling Newearth and starting over. I feel like one of those guys from the old stories... It's overwhelming."

"Now that Doc Mike is laid to rest in a proper ceremony; you've got—"

"By the Divide, wasn't the Governor a bit long—"

"Hello, Governor!"

That smile beats all. I'm not sure how he can make something so intrinsically decent appears so sinister.

"Hello, Cerulean...Peter. It's wonderful to see you here. Terrific speech, Peter, heartfelt and sincere. That's what these people need—to remember their heritage and learn how to work together. No more us and them attitudes, eh?"

"Absolutely. I was just telling Cerulean that my wife, Angelina, has been—"

"Wonderful! Keep up the good work! I must circulate. Got to keep the blood pulsing between races, ha, ha!"

Hand pumps all around.

"If you need me, I'll be in the Capitol. Meetings...planning sessions, you understand. But I'm here for you. Cerulean, don't be a stranger. See if you can talk Sterling into a visit this year, eh?"

"I'll keep that in mind, Governor."

Trip trot... Off he goes. Wonder how long he'll last...?

"Cerulean?"

"Oh, yeah. Sorry, Peter. It's been a long morning."

"I told Angelina I'd help out. You want to visit a while? No work required. You can watch us slave away in the kitchen."

"Charming as that sounds, I can't. I've got one more stop to make before I meet with Roux. There's been some intergalactic action that might need our attention... nothing for you to worry about."

I hope.

"All right... Well, thanks for coming, Cerulean. I know Mom and Dad thought the universe of you and Doctor Mike trusted you, and he didn't trust many beings. Really, we should've been thanking you for this day. Mikestown wouldn't exist if you hadn't—"

"Forget it. I played my part, as did a great many. Say hi to Angelina. I'll visit... soon."

"Hold you to it."

~~~

A gravestone rests under an apple tree, roughly etched with the words: *Anne Smith—Last of Her Kind.* Blinking, Cerulean crouches down and pats the Earth, smoothing the thick grass with a caressing touch. Slowly, he pulls a small leather journal from inside his jacket. He flips to the last page and peers at the words:

The Earth is renewing itself at an astonishing rate. Cerulean has traveled about and told me that it looks like God reinvented the Garden of Eden. I can't help but wonder: Who will live here next? Will they treat the Earth better? Will they treat each other better?

Oh, God, Anne. I hope so.

Invasion

Originally published on The Writings of A. K. Frailey
10/21/2016

—Newearth—

"Angelina! Angelia, where are you?"

Blasted Crestas! What was Raymond thinking? Governor of a multi-race? Idiot! Pound up these steps one last time; I'll probably never see... Damn! Don't think! Just—

"Here, Peter! Everyone's accounted for. Cerulean and Roux are running the— Isn't Paul with you?"

My heart has stopped. Really stopped.

"No. I thought he was helping you."

"He was. But I sent him to find you."

"I've been doing a perimeter check. Everything's down. Crestas certainly know how to blast their way into—"

Tears are filling her eyes. Focus! No tears—not yet...Her voice cracks.

"Where's Paul?"

"He's probably helping with the last of the evacs. Don't worry, honey, I'll find him."

Yeah, sure. The whole planet is blowing to pieces... okay. Stop! Exaggeration won't help. Think!

"Where was he heading?"

Good, she's getting a hold of herself.

"To Capitol Hill."

"You go ahead. I'm sure he's around. Cerulean's probably got everyone else in transport. He snagged a friendly Bhuac trader who was heading

31

home to Helm, but she said she'd take us to Lux first."

"I'm not leaving without my son!"

"Me neither. But it won't help having the two of us wandering— Wait. Holy Hill! I know where he is. Go on! Tell that Bhuac to wait. I'll be right back!"

"Peter!"

~~~

The whole world is falling into enemy hands, but my son wants a last private moment with his hero.

"Paul!"

He's so little for eleven. The Crestas would tower over him like a mountain. But not a hint of fear in those eyes.

"Hey, son, come on! Your mother's worried sick, and Cerulean's holding a Bhuac trading ship for us. We've got to hurry."

"I'm not leaving."

"What? Don't be insane. You're leaving if I have to pick you up and carry you!"

"This is our home. Our planet. The Crestas have no right!"

He's hugging Doctor Mike's statue as if he thinks it'll protect him. So young... So foolish.

"They have much bigger weapons, and they're going to use them. Now quit acting like a child and hurry up. Once their scout teams come this way, they'll take us prisoners...if we're lucky."

"I don't care."

"Well, I care! We can't win. Not this time. We've got to leave—now!"

"Doctor Mike wouldn't. He'd stay and fight."

"By the Divide! He didn't. When humanity lost the first time, he left. And for good reason! There's a time to walk away...or run away and come back later. Right now, we've got a real good reason to run."

"Will we come back...later?"

If my heart keeps falling like this, I'll never find it again.

"I hope so. Come on, son. Your mother is frantic. And Cerulean will have my head."

Good boy... Ah, dang it, he's wiping his eyes with his sleeve. I hate that. I can't feel, I've got to think.

"Stop!"

Damn! Cresta scouts...

"Hold still. We'll not accept resistance."

"Resistance? Look, my hands are up. Put your hands up, Paul. Listen, we're just leaving. No need to worry about us resisting..."

"Hold still."

Oh, God! He's leveling his weapon.

"Tamir! Is that you?"

Thank God, Cerulean! I can breathe again... The scouts not pleased though. Still, Cerulean could charm an Ingoti water rat...

"Do I know you, human?"

Gotta love Cerulean's smile.

"Luxonian. Though I can see how you might make the mistake. Don't you remember me? Cerulean. I was in the leadership council between the Ingal and the Supreme Judges back on Cresta in 04."

"Oh, my apologies. I didn't realize. Are these your—"

"Yes, they're mine. Thank you for holding them. I've been looking for them everywhere. Please, go about your business. I don't think you'll find anyone else. Emergency transportation has been arranged. Next time... you might like to give a little more notice.

"We gave the humans a full day. We're not always so courteous with our enemies."

"Enemies! You're the ene—"

I have to stop my son's mouth. Sorry, but there's a time to shut up. Cerulean glares at him but swings a full grin at the Cresta. Man, he's good.

"Forgive the youth. He's inexperienced."

"Take him or I'll give him an experience."

—*Bhuac Transport*—

Peter leans back with his eyes closed on the cushioned bench with Angelina's sleeping head resting on his shoulder. Paul hunches between crates at his father's feet.

Cerulean steps into the small cargo space. His eyes travel from Peter to Angelina—to Paul. He beckons to Paul in silence.

Paul lumbers to his feet. His red, swollen gaze scrapes the floor.

"Yes, sir?"

Cerulean lifts Paul's chin so that their gaze locks.

"This is not the end. You'll return home. Luxonians will work things out with the Crestas."

34

"And what if another race decides they want Newearth? Will you save us again? There will always be more of them than us."

"True, but defeat isn't the answer. Grieve, as you must, but when you recover, I'll be waiting. There will come a day. You'll return. And I'll come with you."

"Why?"

"Because...it's my home too."

I Never Had a Son

Originally published on The Writings of A. K. Frailey
11/4/2016

—Planet Lux—

A courtyard dominated by a two-story fountain and decorated with generous fauna wafting in a gentle breeze as cloud sprays reflect every color in the spectrum.

Cerulean stands before the fountain, silent and alone.

I miss Viridian. Or rather, I miss what I hoped we'd have together—my son, following in my footsteps or perhaps forging a new path together.

Must all such dreams die? Surely not...

Anne had a second chance with her daughter, and Peter has grown closer to his son. Not all families are doomed to a hideous fate. But me? My father has been long gone, and I'll never have another son.

"Cerulean?"

"Yes, Judge Sterling. What can I do for you, sir?"

Surprise.... He's in his human form, with his matching white suit and beard...looking as dashing as any aging Luxonian with delusions of—

"Supreme Judge. Formality, I know, but we must keep up appearances."

"Yes, Supreme Judge. Sterling."

"Odd. When you say it—never mind. I've come to inform you that a council has been appointed to discuss the Human Question...again."

"Sir?"

"Don't think I haven't noticed your efforts on their behalf."

"I believe I told you my concerns up front."

"Yes, and I was listening. You look doubtful."

"You never appeared interested."

"Humanity has proven useful. I'm not ignorant of their worth. I simply needed to understand how involved the Cresta was going to be."

"Now that Ingots, the Uanyi, and Bhuacs have staked their claims—is it involved enough?"

"Stop scowling, Cerulean. If you'd appear like a proper Luxonian, I'd feel more comfortable."

"But I wouldn't."

"So, I've noticed. In any case, I have a friend...shall we say a benign enemy who—"

"You mean the reporter—Lang?"

"You know her?"

"She's notorious."

"Yes, well, we have an understanding. She lies to me... I lie to her... And we understand each other perfectly."

"What lies has she been telling you now?"

"She was kind enough to inform me that Crestas have outlawed all crossbreed experimentation, that the Ingots have no interest in Newearth, that the Uanyi plan on relocating on the dark side of the Divide, and that the Bhuacs are quite happy being decimated."

"With enemies like her, who needs friends?"

"My thoughts exactly."

"So... What's the next step?"

"We must regain our position on Newearth, but that means we need an alliance everyone can agree with."

"An impossible challenge."

"It's *your* challenge, Cerulean. Come up with a plan, think of a way to present it to the Supreme Council so that they see how it benefits Luxonian society, in fact, make it seem like their idea. Then return to Newearth and make it happen."

I can feel sweat trickling down my back. What I wouldn't do for an ice-cold—anything. "I can't do this alone."

"You won't. Roux will accompany you to Newearth. You'll make friends—"

Uh, oh, that one-of-a-kind, tormented stare....

"You always do. Find allies; convince them that it is in their best interest if we all work together.

"It will be."

"See? You've convinced me already."

Odd. I never noticed that his smile has a certain charm. "When is the council meeting?"

"Tomorrow, early. Come ready for battle. Act like it's the end of life as we know it—"

"I've already used that argument. It only works once."

"True."

By the Divide, he's pacing the walkway, stroking his beard like a human patriarch of old.

"Lang advised me that since Newearth is so *poor* in natural resources, there isn't a merchant within a million light years who'd be interested in it."

"Merchants? They're as dangerous as politicians."

"Don't be ridiculous. Merchants are thieves and liars, but they have honest souls. They know perfectly well that war shrinks the profit margin. The Luxonian Council—"

"Supreme Luxonian Council."

"Yes, of course, they want happy merchants because happy merchants protect our assets."

"I see."

Strange that I never noticed this side of Sterling before. How could I have missed it?

"Thank you, sir. I was nearly out of options."

"I know. I do have eyes...never mind. I must attend to other Supreme Judge business."

"Of course."

"Cerulean?"

Deep breath. He's staring again. "Yes?"

"I never had a son."

Forget ice cold; my mouth just went as dry as the dark side of the Divide. "If you had, he'd probably have been just like you."

Exactly. But you—you're nothing like me.

"Sir?"

"I never wanted a son, Cerulean.... See you in the council chamber.

Alcina's Journal
Originally published on The Writings of A. K. Frailey
11/18/2016

—Newearth—

Year 25

It's been five years now since Cerulean arrived with his Inter-Alien Alliance agreement. Governor Sharp met her match in him, that's for sure. I wonder who'll take over now?

Lordy, I'm tired. Way too tired to take notice of all the recent upheavals. I do care but…. Uh oh, here comes someone in an all-fired rush.

"Alcina, there's been an accident. Hurry. We'll need your healing bag."

So much for quiet time and contemplation.

I step out of my little herb shop, and who do I find but my friend, 'Roux-to-the-Rescue'…again. Even for a Luxonian, he's fast. And he's too handsome for his own good…well, for my good.

"I'm coming! Let me grab my stuff and check something."

Dash in. Grab a cloak, my bag, and check— anything on the boiler? Nope. Oops. Got to strain those berries before the ants—

"Alcina?"

Rush, rush! I'm coming! And dashing right—

"Sorry. Didn't see you in the doorway."

Even when he's perturbed, he's handsome. Sigh.

"So—Who is it this time? An Ingoti construction worker fell off his high-rise? An Uanyi merchant tackle a thieving intergalactic trader? Don't tell me—a Cresta has blown a tentacle to smithereens in one of his new labs?"

I'm jogging along to keep up, trying not to sound like I'm completely breathless. Building my shop out here in the wilds of Westland has its advantages, but not so much when I'm in a hurry.

"Sarcasm doesn't become you, Alcina. Healers are supposed to maintain their professional dignity at all times—with all races. It's in your creed—or code—or something."

"Huh. Must've missed that part. Roux! Would you please slow down? I'm not made of light so I can't move as fast."

"Sorry. It'd be easier if I could—"

"Don't even think about it."

"We've improved our transportation methods. Really. You'll hardly even notice..."

"No, thanks. I've buried enough transportation failures to give me a strong devotion to pedestrian travel."

"You can't live in the OldEarth past."

"I can try. Well, sort of. Though, I must say; I'm deeply in love with my whirligig."

"Whirligig?"

"It does all my laundry, dries it, and leaves it folded on—oh, never mind. Where are we rushing off to anyway?"

Roux didn't even blink. "The past."

Speaking of sarcasm...

"You really ought to spend more time with the Bhuacs. They love riddles and you'd have a gorgeous time figuring your way out of their labyrinths. I hear their settlement in Song—"

Roux is still not blinking. No emotion whatsoever.

"Been there. Nearly died. Not my best memory."

I'm trying not to express my jumbled feeling on every fiber of my face. "Oooh-kay. So, you want to tell me what's going on?"

"Simple case. A new community named Amens, a guy broke something in his back while building a house. They want to keep close to nature, so they use the old ways and only natural resources. You should get along great. They'll love your plant-of-the-day shop—natural remedies and all."

"I'm an herbologist."

"You're an OldEarth naturalist."

"Why do you make that seem like some kind of insult?"

"It's not intended. Look, I respect what you do, but you can't ignore the reality of living in a world with universal technology."

"Who's ignoring? I told you about my whirligig and look, see, I'm advanced."

It's a tab bit embarrassing holding out my arm for inspection like this, but hey, a comp-insert is pretty blinking impressive.

Lordy, he's holding my arm...and looking me in the eye. Sheesh. He dropped my arm like I'm made of ice.

"Where'd you get that?"

"Cerulean gave it to me. He said we needed a better way to stay in touch, I mean, in communication. You know how he is."

"Yeah, I know Cerulean well indeed. Listen, I'm just going to shorten this little jaunt by a hair's breadth if you don't mind."

"A hair's breadth? What does—?"

"Wahhhh...."

Now Roux looks smug. Seriously smug. "Here we are."

I'm checking my heart...Thank God! It's still beating. Honestly, I'm grateful I still exist, corporeally speaking. "Roux! I outta shoot you. How dare you—"

Uh ho, he's grinning. Dang, I can't be mad at him when he smiles like that. Deep breath. Regain some semblance of dignity.

"I apologize. I'm just afraid this guy will die while we're traipsing through Newearth's natural elements."

"Okay. Good reason. I'm looking around but I don't see much. Just an old barn and a few outbuildings."

"That barn is bigger than it looks, and it's the center of the Amens community. Here, follow me."

~~~

We're inside a huge structure, like nothing I've ever seen before. It's a luminous, pulsing green with lofts and little niches all over the place, built of some kind of plant structure; it could be a tree, but it's not like any vegetation I've ever encountered before. It feels...alive.

Roux strides up and knocks, the bold fellow that he is. "Hello? It's me, Roux. I've brought—"

"Oh, Roux! Thanks for coming."

Hmmm. A Bhuac. Charming little beings, elusive though. Wonder what...?

By the look on his face, Roux isn't here to exchange pleasantries. "Shira? Where's the patient?"

"I'm sorry for troubling you, Roux, but he's passed on. The damage was too great, and his family didn't want too much intervention."

"I tried to get here as quick as I could. I brought a neighbor of yours, Alcina, the herbologist."

Those luminous eyes! Bhuacs are gorgeous no matter what shape they take. But she's so sad...touched.

"Alcina? Yes, we know of you. Song of Wisdom admires your work."

The Song of Wisdom? Seen me? And I failed to notice? "Sorry, we didn't get here in time. It was my fault. I'm slow—"

"Don't trouble your soul. The Amens have great faith. We have found strength in each other. I will introduce you. They are in mourning now."

"Certainly. Is there anything I can do for you...or anyone?"

"Thank you, child. I'll inform them of your arrival and preparations for burial will begin immediately. You may assist in preparing the body if you like. I am sure they would appreciate your skill."

Skill? "I can't heal the dead."

"No. But you can ease the passage for those who remain. You have buried many, and your respect for the body is admirable. Let me know what you need, and I'll procure the materials."

She's turned her powerful laser-like gaze on Roux now.

"Roux? Would you inform Cerulean that we need his assistance?"

"Cerulean? Sure. Why? I thought the guy fell off the roof."

"Only after he was shot with a Dustbuster. There's trouble ahead."

Poor Roux. It's never easy being a hero in a universe of villains. Sigh...I've been hidden away—too old to notice the troubles of our time— too young to care... But now...

"Alcina?"

"Yes."

"You're needed."

That I am. Sigh.

Eldars—My Father's Vision

Originally published on The Writings of A. K. Frailey
12/2/2016

—Planet Crestar—

"The ancients among us have always been called the Eldar, son, though considering how strangely some Crestonians behave, 'Peculiar' might be a more appropriate title. Here, give me that dissecting knife. The thin one on the left. Yes, thank you."

My stomach always lurched at the first incision. Sometimes I wondered if I was really a full-blooded Cresta. I gripped the edge of the steel table with one tentacle, passed the knife to my father with another, and wiped my face with a third.

"One has to pass the fifth-century mark to be assigned to the Eldar circle, but since advancements in health and fitness have increased our lifespan, nearly every Cresta has a good chance of becoming Elder, at least for a time—dark waters! I don't think he died naturally. Look at that green gelatinous mass."

"What does it mean, Taugron?"

"It means that we have a traitor among us. Don't look so surprised. Crestas are devoted to science—not to each other."

"What are you going to do?"

"Dig deeper of course. Now, about your question. The Eldar believe that Cresta is one of the strongest races in existence."

"But you don't?"

"Pull that flap of skin back, please. And open a sample case. I'm going to do a little more research into this poison. It looks like it grew from a seed. I wonder if was served on land or in water..."

"Would it make any difference?"

"Of course. Think! Our senses are nearly perfect in water. Normally we'd pick up an anomaly in a matter of seconds. But on land, we're much more vulnerable. Also, most aliens we associate with are terrestrials...."

"But you said a traitor. A non-Cresta can't be a traitor."

"There are many kinds of traitors. Even a well-intentioned Cresta can become a traitor. It all depends on how things turn out... Ah, I see I have confused you. You see, I do not hold with all the beliefs of our Eldars, and some would label me a traitor if given the chance."

"Why? What do you believe?"

"See? The pod is still attached and it has a smooth, blue coating, much like the Winnieria seed found in shallow waters. It's completely harmless so no one would care if they swallowed one or a dozen. But this...this is the work of—"

"A monster."

"No, on the contrary, a very clever mind. Take a look at the face. This dead Cresta is nothing but a shell of his former self, but once upon a time, he was a great servant of our race. But he was vulnerable. We all are. If we had new blood, fresh ideas, and adaptive physiology, we could survive even the most nefarious schemes."

"Is that your plan? Your good intention?"

"Yes, though nothing really grand. I'd simply like to crossbreed our kind with another race and prove it can be done successfully. I'd start with a human; they may be fragile, but they have certain adaptabilities that intrigue me. Eventually, we'll be able to blend our mental acumen with Ingoti strength, Uanyi creativity, and Bhuac adaptability. We would become—"

"Invincible."

"Near enough. Even he-I-won't-name would be impressed. In fact...never mind. You're too young. Someday perhaps. But, in the meantime, take this cadaver to the incinerator. Now that I have the key to his death, we can get on with our work."

"Will I become an Eldar, Father?"

"Perhaps. If you live long enough. But remember, son, it isn't about living a long life...it's about advancing. If you don't advance...you might as well be dead."

~~~

"Taug?"

"I'm here."

"Are you all right? You look upset."

"No, nothing of the sort. You may go now. The incinerator will do the rest."

"If you're sure.... Taug, your father will be missed. He was a noble Eldar with fine vision— even in the darkest water."

"Thank you."

"Perhaps you will carry on his vision?"

"Perhaps. Go ahead now. I need to send a message..."

48

Attention: Ingal Department of
Internal-Security.
Private.

*The remains are clean and disposed of. There is
no sign of the traitor's work left on Crestar, and the
lab has been dismantled. I am, as always, ever at
your service.*

Taug, son of Taugron

Life of Gorth—Fate of a Weapon Maker

Originally published on The Writings of A. K. Frailey
12/16/2016

Planet—Ingilium

Moglum's Land Base Rental

Renter Gorth is practicing war games on the back lot…

"I will not die! At least not today! So take that! And that! And that!"

Bam! Fizzzt!

"Gorth! Hold on, would you? You're turning my back lot into a crater. I know you're a lean, mean, fighting machine—but please—I need some space that isn't constantly being bombarded with shrapnel. My poor nerves—"

"What a landlord! Where's your Ingilum spirit, Moglum? Your mama should've packed you off on one of those slave transports."

"Nice. Real nice, Gorth. Now shut up and listen. Someone from the Imperium just sent a message—"

"From the Imperium? For me?"

"Yeah, and if you're being transferred, you better fix this mess before you leave!"

Imperium Central Office for Interplanetary Security

Hologram message coming through...

"Citizen Iz, secretary for the Imperium, can I help you?"

"Oh, hi, it's me...I mean...this is citizen Gorth. You sent a message—"

"Gorth! Yes, thank you for checking in so quickly. Good news. We've been watching your progress and decided that this is the time to support your... unique skills."

"Um. What does that mean exactly?"

"Listen, Gorth, there's a new threat. We've received secret information that the Cresta are planning an invasion... and they won't be coming alone."

"Annihilate! Really? This is big. How can I help? I mean with the weapons' ban and all..."

"The ban has been lifted. Your research may continue where you left off. In fact, the Imperium is prepared to assist you by any means necessary."

Silence.

"Gorth?"

"Oh, yeah... I just had to get back on my feet...I sorta fell over. Honestly, I never expected this. You know, weapons are my passion. I live to evaporate. It's what I dream about. After the ban, I had to be content with just blowing—"

"We understand. That's why you have been chosen. You're gifted and if it hadn't been for interplanetary pressure, we'd never have agreed to that infernal... Never mind. The fact is, you are now reinstated. Fully. Get back to work, Gorth."

Three moon cycles later...back at Moglum's Land Base Rental

Moglum and Gorth sit hunched on a steel bench as they lean over a long table strewn with various weapon and weapon parts.

Gorth holds up a small, smooth, and rounded handheld devise, his chest puffs with pride. "I'm calling it the Evaporator."

Moglum frowns. "Nah... Come on Gorth; don't be stupid. That name's already been taken. It blew the entire watching audience to smithereens. Don't you remember? It was on every hologram from here to the Cresta Divide."

"Musta repressed it. Hmmm... I'm not so good at naming things. Any ideas?"

"How about the Destroyer? The Atomizer? The Dustbuster?"

"Hey, I like that. The Dustbuster! I'll call it the Dustbuster I. I mean, I've done about a kazillion of these things but nobody needs to know that."

"Go down in history as the greatest weapon maker of all time... Brilliant. Oh, and when you get paid... You *are* getting paid for this right?"

"Sure. The Imperium said they'd give me what I deserve."

"Well, then, you'll be in a position to rebuild the back lot. I was thinking of turning it into something like that resort on the South Sea. You know, the one with all the foliage and females..."

"Yeah. Yeah... I'll get to it. But first I got to present this to the Imperium. See what they think."

"You'll be a hero. No doubt about it. I always said you'd make the Ingot name great again."

"Ah... Just following my passion."

—Universal News Today—

It has been verified that the missing inventor of the Dustbuster I, Gorth, has finally been tracked to the back lot of Moglum's Land Base Rental. Apparently, his newest weapon had been used against him and then stolen.

The Imperium requests that any information concerning Gorth's demise be sent directly to their Central Security Office.

On the interplanetary front, it appears that Crestas are once again up to no good....

Lugg the Mighty and the Oskilth Civil War

Originally published on The Writings of A. K. Frailey
12/30/2016

—Planet Crestar—
Cresta Research Laboratory for Advanced Security

Cresta: A techno-organic race from the planet Crestar with long, soft bodies, tentacles, and large, watery eyes. They speak in a synthesized voice, and their large "brain sack" lays hidden behind a spiral shell. They wear breathing helms when not on their own water-based planet.

Ingot: A cyborg race from the planet Ingilium that wears bulky techno-organic armor and breather helms built directly into their bodies.

Lugg leaned over a tray of medical-type instruments.

A fellow Cresta lumbered over and tapped him with a tentacle. "Lugg? Lugg!"

"Oh? Yes. Can I help you?"

"It's time to eat. You coming?"

"Already?"

"Yes, Lugg. Please, you'll wither away to nothing if you keep working like this."

"Heh, heh... I doubt that. But, well... I guess you're right. Here, let me just—"

"Put it down Lugg, or I'll be forced to call for help."

"Yes, yes. I'm coming..."

Lugg and his companion shuffled down a long grey tunnel on cushioned flipper-like feet, their tentacles swayed at their sides.

A large well-stocked pool behind a thick glass wall swirled with murky sea vegetation and swimming creatures.

Three other Crestas flipped their heads out of the water and grinned down at the two. "Come in and feast a while."

Lugg's companion climbed up a ladder and leaned over the pool, his eyes glowed in anticipation. He darted a glance back at Lugg. "Aren't you coming?"

Lugg stared at a fish swimming in the murky depths; he heaved a sigh and turned around.

"Hey! Come back! You'll die if you don't eat."

Lugg lumbered away.

~~~

A huge Ingot lay slumped on the laboratory floor.

Lugg held a flexible disk in his tentacle, aimed it at the Ingot.

His Cresta companion stared at him through wide, amazed eyes. "I never knew you had it in you, Lugg. For such a pacifist, that was quite a move. I thought he'd wreck the place."

"Don't be silly. I'm always prepared for invaders. I've been working on this weapon for years."

"You? Create a weapon? I thought you were working on a new breathing mask. You can't even eat meat. Your vegetables are served cold—on a plate for darkness' sake—and far from their natural environment."

Lugg held up the disk and grinned, though his eyes remained soft and serious. "This is the most effective weapon ever created. When this Ingot awakes, he'll feel weak for hours, and all aggression will have left his body. He won't want to fight."

"You have altered his—"

"Brain activity. He'll be useless as a fighter for months, even years, and he certainly won't come here again. If we use this weapon judiciously, neither will any others. All wars will end."

"How? I mean; I'm stunned. When did you discover that this...this thing worked?"

"Right after I tried it on myself."

Universal Reports
OSKILTH WAR AT AN END

The island of Oskilth has finally been subdued through the use of the Mighty Lugg Stinger. Unfortunately, the Taser's mind-altering abilities affected so many active Cresta soldiers that the Crestar governing body, Ingal, has decreed that the Mighty Lugg Stinger is too dangerous to remain in existence.

The scientist behind the mighty invention was ordered to destroy it, but apparently, he and the Taser have both disappeared...

~ ~ ~

A young Cresta entered a small, dim, hole-in-the-wall laboratory. "Lugg? Sir? Are you here?"

Lugg shuffled forward from a dark corner and met the youth. "Hmmm? Can I help you?"

"Oh, hi, sir. I live down the hall. My mother sent me over to give this to you. It's cold sea-pie. We heard that it's something you like. She just wants to thank you."

Lugg's large, luminous, green eyes gleamed in the dim light. "Me? Why?"

"Well, my brother was slated for the next trip to Oskilth. He's of age and was set to fight—"

"Ah, yes. So many were sent over...."

"Well, now, since the war is over, he's being sent to Cresta Labs for adaptive technologies—something to do with making better breathing masks."

"Honorable service. I'm happy for him."

"Anyway, mother is real glad, and I am too. Maybe things will be different when I am of age."

"I hope so. But you know, I'm not really here."

"Yes, of course. Mother figured it out, but she'll keep your secret safe. Do you have the Mighty Lugg Stinger still?"

"It was stolen."

"Oh. Sorry."

"Don't be. Sometimes things need to be stolen."

"Really? I never.... Well, I better go. Mother said to tell you that she's sorry you had to leave."

"It was a small price to pay."

"Enjoy the pie. Bye."

Lugg watched the youth lumber away. He stared at the pie, grinned, and then lumbered back to his worktable. He lay the pie down next to a new, very different looking weapon.

Omega's Homecoming

Originally published on The Writings of A. K. Frailey
1/27/2017

—Mystery Planet—

Across the darkness, a voice called.

"Father?"

A circle of light appeared and, in the center, stood a young man dressed in a short, burgundy tunic, black leggings, and a royal purple cape with a dashing short sword stuck in his belt. He bowed low.

Another man appeared, older and grayer, wearing a long, black cloak over a white tunic. The elder nodded to the younger, a half-smile glinting through his eyes. "Obsessed aren't you, Last One?"

The young man grinned and, waving one hand majestically against the outer darkness, a humble village appeared with a medieval castle perched on the top of a low hill.

"An obsession you once shared, Father." The son shuffled along the dirt path leading to the hill. "Call me Omega, now. It sounds so much more...hopeful. After all, *your* last is not *my* end." A grin took the edge off his bitterness.

The father trod along at his son's side; his hands clasped behind his back. "True. Though we all face an end—sometime. Remember that." He glanced around at the villagers bustling amongst myriad thatched huts and fenced yards, hurrying to their daily business, offering low bows of obeisance as he passed. He tipped his head in a lordly fashion, earning wide-eyed curtsies from the women and squared shoulders from the men. "Besides, I was never obsessed. Not like you. Interested. Merely interested." He glanced at the castle as he climbed the cobbled incline. "Your mother awaits."

Omega twirled around as he locked his gaze on a pretty maiden. Tearing himself away, he trotted after his father. "Humans are my favorite. I believe they always will be. I'm making them my specialty."

The father grunted as he twitched a branch off of a nearby tree. Peering at the stick, it suddenly transformed from a ragged twig into a beautifully carved walking staff. He tapped the staff on the paving stones leading to the castle gates—huge, ornate affairs with burly soldiers guarding each side. "You have many races to choose from—don't be too hasty to pick a favorite. Keep your mind open."

Throwing his arms wide, Omega appeared to embrace the entire village. "Oh, Father! Humans are the best. Cresta minds are so narrow and small, forever focused on science, pretending to be logical while lying to themselves; Ingots and Uanyi are like children inside mechanical bodies, and the Bhuacs, well, they are intriguing. So versatile. Pity they've been decimated so often. They're not nearly as resilient as humans."

A bell tolled from the castle's highest tower. Both men looked up, the father with a sigh and the son with adoration. The father waved his stick at the village throng. "Humans retain their barbarism for just such a purpose. They could never survive without it."

Omega raced up the last paces to the gates and turned before the guards, his arms wide, a gleam shining through his eyes. "And what are we—without zoos and life studies? Surely those that live in our villages would consider us nothing more than oppressors—if they knew."

The father stepped past his son and gestured to the guards, who promptly pulled open the heavy gates. He spoke over his shoulder. "If they knew. My point exactly." He waved his son into the inner courtyard. Pages and squires bustled, leading horses to open stalls while stately nobles stood aside, clustered in private consultation. The sound of a hammer striking metal on the left told the tale of other industries near at hand.

"But, Father, they must know, in their own way—"

"They know they are oppressed because they struggle against it always—even when it isn't there." The father stared ahead as a woman appeared in the doorway of the keep. A youthful woman wearing an ornamental dress with a golden belt tied around her waist and thick hair falling across her shoulders smiled at them.

The father hurried his steps.

Omega hustled at his father's side. "One day, Father, I will test your theory. I'll create one of my own and—"

His father stopped and spun on his heel, glowering. "You can create nothing! Don't speak like a fool. Your studies have made you forget your limits."

Chastened, Omega lowered his gaze. "I just want to discover how far their natures will expand...."

With a huff of impatience, the father brushed his son's words aside. "Someday you will realize that not all questions need to be answered. In fact, it is best if they aren't." He gazed at the woman; his scowl instantly replaced by a gleam of joy. He stared into the woman's sparkling eyes. "I've brought him home—at last."

Omega rushed forward and embraced the woman. "Sorry it took me so long, Mother; there was so much to see and do!"

The woman threw back her head and laughed as she wound her arms around her son in a warm embrace. "You never change! Always insatiable! Come, I've prepared a feast, just as you like it, warriors and roasted venison abound!"

Omega, with his arm around his mother, entered the confines of the keep. His father sighed as he looked after them, shaking his head and murmuring, "He'd devour the universe—if he could."

Omega's Creation

Originally published on The Writings of A. K. Frailey
2/10/2017

—Mystery Planet—

"Your name is Justice." Omega stroked his chin, his lips twitching in uncertainty. "Hmmm...not quite. Too *Pilgrim's Progress* for my taste. Let's see. Honesty? Truth? Oh, help; I might as well be naming an OldEarth compendium on the virtues of... virtue. How dreary!"

The figure of a young woman with long, black hair, dressed in a form-fitting, dark blue, bodysuit, lay on a table, her hands clasped over her chest like the remains of a dearly departed. Omega clapped his hands in frustration. "The joys of creation! Even God Himself left the naming to his creatures." Omega snapped his fingers, a light in his eyes. "She'll tell me."

Running his hand over the woman's head, he closed his eyes in concentration.

The woman stirred. Her blue eyes blinked open.

Omega stepped back, one hand over his mouth as if to stifle a laugh—or a scream.

The woman turned her head, her gaze running over the figure before her. A frown formed between her brows. "Who—?"

Omega stepped forward; his hand extended for assistance. "Here, let me help you." With a gentle touch, he pulled the woman to a sitting position. Bowing in a courtly manner, he smiled. "My name is Omega. At least that's what my father calls me.

But since you are my original creation, I suppose you must call me—creator."

"Creator?" The woman shifted slightly as her gaze scoured the silent, still laboratory. "Why am I here?"

Omega's eyes followed hers, and he frowned. "Yes, well, my laboratory isn't much yet, I'll admit. But this is not your destination. I've arranged for a transport to take you beyond the Divide where you'll find...employment."

The woman threw her legs over the table and clenched the edge. "I am a—"

Omega shook his head. "Not sure yet. To be honest, Father warned me about this. I have a tendency to rush in where fools fear to tread." With a sigh, Omega took the woman's hand and helped her off the table. "But don't be afraid. You have the strength of twenty humans, the data banks of six species, and enough moral code to ensure your survival."

"You will direct me?"

Omega shook his head, his gaze lowered. "No. That would ruin everything. If I'm to learn anything, you must discover yourself. But—" He looked up and grinned. "I'm working on another one like you, a male this time. He's been a challenge, but he'll come out all right in the end, I dare say." Omega led the woman to a doorway, still clasping her hand. "Strange, I hate to let you go, though I know I must."

The woman stopped on the threshold. "Who am I?"

Omega rubbed his brow. "You are what humans fear most. I was going to name you Justice but that rankled my sensibilities." He led her across the threshold and down a long corridor. Other beings, Crestas, Ingots, and two Uanyi passed without comment. When they came upon a large tunnel, Omega led her to an open-sided vehicle and stood by as she perched on the edge of a seat. "It's a short ride to the central station. Busy place, but I enjoy the bustle of activity." Various beings entered the open vehicle. A Cresta lumbered over and gripped a central pole with his long tentacles while two slim, Uanyis with their soft, rubbery exoskeletons slumped on a seat together, chatting in their own language.

The woman stared at her hands and then at the others. Omega watched her and sighed. When the vehicle stopped outside a docking bay, Omega nudged her forward. A huge window separated them from the stationary ships, docked for repairs or loading for their next foray into space. The woman stared at the masses of beings hustling all around her. "I see Ingots, Crestas, Uanyi, and Bhuacs—but none like me."

"No, you are part android and part human. Humanity is not ready for you—yet. It's your privilege to discover the larger universe before being introduced to your other half. I'll be delighted to see what you make of yourself." He pointed to the largest ship. "You will travel on that one, The Mercantile. A trader in need of protection has hired you." Omega gripped her hand and gazed into her eyes. "There will be trouble ahead; war brews in the hearts of these beings. But I'm sure you will manage." Omega peered deeper into Justine's steady gaze. He smiled with a relieved chuckle. "Yes, you'll do fine. There's something ethereal about you." Caressing her cheek, he mused. "Justine... Santana...holy justice. That'll be your name. Whether you live up to it or not— will be up to you."

A blaring noise swept across the loading dock. Omega took Justine's hand and led her forward. "Time to meet your future."

As Omega stood back, Justine ascended the boarding tube. She looked back once, clear-eyed and confident, before she disappeared into the interior.

Omega waved. "I'll be watching you."

Save Our People From Despair

Originally published on The Writings of A. K. Frailey
3/24/2017

—Planet Helm—

Despair is an ugly thing. When my mother sent me away after the invasion—little did she dream of what she exiled me to—hopeless dread and futile guilt. With her hands, she pushed me away, yet with her heart, she clung to me.

"Come back when you can; save us if you can. But at least one Bhuac must survive. And it must be you!"

I did as she demanded. I took the transport on docking bay one-one-four and headed out into the universe and away from certain Bhuaci destruction. I was protected only by a gruff, Ingot merchant named Buford, who needed someone to blame when things went wrong, which, with his clumsy skills, they often did. I accepted every menial job: collating orders, checking the ship's inventory, noticing when things went missing, and even tracking down a guilty thief once. I was a Bhuac of all-work-and-no-play and served in every role imaginable, servant, advisor, director, detective, even guard on occasion. Being a shapeshifter, I could cover my quaking insecurities with hulking forms and menacing fangs.

But I never played the part I longed to return to—Faye, a gentle, beloved daughter. Even as a friend, I would have felt some satisfaction. But

Buford was not interested in friends. He was interested in units, the more, the better. Profit was his closest kin.

Then one day, we headed toward a planet I had never been to, a rising star on the horizon, called Newearth. Buford told me its colorful history, the demise of Oldearth, the Luxonians' protection, the Cresta invasion, the Inter-Alien Alliance Commission. Something in me stirred for the first time in uncounted cycles. I longed to visit this new horizon, but Buford changed his mind, and we veered toward the Divide and a greater profit margin.

I waited.

Then a new opportunity struck. A traveler boarded—a hidden figure who merely said that he was heading to Newearth. His name was Gabriel. He appeared human, as I did on most occasions, but I sensed he was Bhuaci, like me. Knowing our own planet's desolation and our sister planet's demise, I could understand his desire for secrecy.

Gabriel paid Buford well to take him to Newearth. My imagination stirred, dead hopes rekindled, but I could not break free of my employer. How could I? I had no one to turn to, nowhere to go.

As we approached Newearth, Gabriel tossed a satchel he always carried over his shoulder and offered Buford his final payment. Buford held out his datapad, tapping his foot. He had contacted a Cresta merchant who was to meet him on the other side of the planet. I stood by, watching, an unnamed grief wringing my soul. Then Gabriel surprised us both.

"Here, that should cover all costs."

Buford glanced at the data-pad ready to pass it to me, when his eyes widened, and he pulled it close and read it again. "What's this? Trying to play some kind of game?"

Gabriel's brows furrowed. "I never play games."

"But it's too much, by half or more. We agreed on twenty-five and this here's near fifty. You're Interventionist, aren't you? Trying to catch me out! Well, it can't be done; I'm an honest—"

Gabriel waved Buford's concerns away. "Nothing of the sort. It's just that I plan on taking your hired help with me. She'll be quite useful on Newearth, and you'll find another—"

"Not one as good! By the Divide, I'm not letting her go. She's going with me to—"

Gabriel faced me and bid me come closer. I was in my favorite fairy-like form, lithe with large, almond eyes and shining, golden hair. I stepped nearer, hardly daring to breathe. Gabriel smiled down at me and clasped my hand. "You're one of our own. So few of us left." He turned to Buford. "If you don't release her, I'll charge you with enslaving a Bhuaci against her will. I happen to know someone on the Inter-Alien Alliance Com—"

"Take her, then! Good riddance. I only hired her for pity's sake. She's so timid and all. You'll find that out." He looked slyly out of the corner of his eyes. "And when you tire of her, send her back. I'm too soft, I know, but I'd hate to see her come to ruin on some dirty street."

With a nod, Gabriel led me toward the debarkation tube. I had nothing to carry with me, so I accepted his direction and started away. I only looked back once. Buford had turned away.

When we arrived on the Newearth Main Street, I was overwhelmed by the bright, bustling energy all around. This was like no planet I had ever seen before. I thought my heart would burst with excitement. Gabriel continued to hold my hand as we scurried across the street and up to a tall building with large, gleaming windows.

I stared up at the brilliant structure set against the blazing, blue sky. "Where are we going?"

"Home. Temporary of course, but it will do until you become accustomed to your new role."

My gaze dropped from the building to Gabriel's face. "My role?"

Gabriel bent down at my side. "The one your mother assigned you—savior of Bhuaci." As the sun beat down upon his golden head, a light shone in my eyes. I could barely see him, but I never forgot his words. "I'm your mother's friend and your friend too. Your family sent me. I've been searching all these years. Now, finally, you will save our people from despair."

My eyes filled with tears. I had a friend, a home, and a mission, too. But who would save me from despair?

This Devil Doesn't Lie

Originally published on The Writings of A. K. Frailey
4/7/2017

—Newearth—

Clare flopped down on her bed with her arms spread wide and her legs dangling over the edge. A black cat jumped forward and curled up on the pillow, nearly blanketing Clare's face. With a nudge, Clare pushed the shorthaired feline aside. "Hey, you, pillow-stealer!"

The cat blinked, yawned expansively, and then laid its head back on the pillow.

After slapping the light panel off, Clare nudged the cat to the side and wiggled contentedly under a thick blanket. "Ah, nothing like a well-deserved rest after a long, hard day's work." She closed her eyes, murmuring, "Nothing you'd know anything about."

Only a faint moonlight shone through the window, illuminating the sharp edges of her dresser and a couple wall pictures. With the pleasant sensation of drifting into dreamland, Clare's lips curled into a contented smile.

"Clare."

Clare sat bolt upright. She knew she had heard a sound, her name, but who— She blinked and swallowed, her mouth half open. Peering over the sleeping cat, she braced herself. Nothing. She frowned. Her eyes scoured the darkened room as she tensed for the slightest noise. Silence. With a shake, she gripped the blanket and pulled it tight around her shoulders, and lay back down.

It took a little time to release the tension in her body, but soon her muscles relaxed, and she felt a comforting drowsiness claiming her.

"Clare, I must speak with you."

Shooting like a star across the room, Clare was in her robe and slippers before the cat could slip out the door. She swiped her Dustbuster off the dresser and held it firmly with both hands, aiming at the door. "Who are you?"

A long, weary sigh floated like a ghostly scent through the room.

Clare twirled like a ballet dancer, nearly falling off balance. "What the hell?"

"You've forgotten me? I'm affronted. Saddened, actually. I thought seeing me in person would forever sear me into your memory."

Clare lowered the weapon as her formerly pink face blanched of all color. She slapped at the light panel, illuminating the room. "Damn you!"

"I certainly hope not. Unkind, Clare, very unkind!"

"Show yourself!"

Omega appeared in the center of the room. He stood, dressed like an ordinary Newearth human in loose-fitting, black pants, a light blue sweater, and brown loafers. He lifted his arms and twirled like a model on a showcase runway. "Like it? The very epitome of ordinary. I'm trying to blend in, you see."

Clare raised the Dustbuster again. "Why are you here?"

Omega snapped his fingers and the Dustbuster instantly rematerialized as a stuffed animal—a pink and purple giraffe. "Please, stop playing ridiculous games. I have very little time, and I have a score to settle with you."

Clare stared at the stuffed animal, her eyes widening. She threw it against the wall and glared at Omega. "A score with me? I should be the one—"

"Yes, of course! You made it quite clear in the courtroom, before my nearest and dearest, what you thought of me. A *devil,* you called me. You have no idea, Clare, really, no idea at all."

Pressing her hands together as if to hold them back from spontaneous combustion, Clare shook her head. "You play with us like toys." She glanced at the stuffed animal that now lay forlornly in the corner.

Omega huffed. "Because you don't understand, you lie about me. How human! I simply won't stand for it any longer. Why do you hate me? Or rather, why do you *think* you hate me?"

Clare's breathing rose and fell in shuddering gasps. "You—killed—my—parents! And then you wanted to analyze my suffering—"

"Lies, lies and more lies. I did nothing of the sort. On the contrary, I saved your life. Your parents died of poisoned stew, true, but to be quite honest, I don't know who poisoned them. But I did realize that someone intended to wipe out your whole family, so I went out of my way to make certain that you were safe. I watched over you like a devoted father hen." Omega paused, one eyebrow rising. "I'm not sure that works." He shrugged. "Anyway, when I asked you questions, it was to get to the bottom of the mystery—to protect you."

Clare stood rooted to the floor. A flush spread over her cheeks. "It can't be. You never cared."

"I always cared."

"No!"

Omega stamped his foot. "I don't have time for this! I have to leave soon, and I have a request to make."

Clare stared stone still and silent.

Omega stepped closer, his gaze boring into Clare's. "Watch over Justine and the child. That silly idiot named her Aurora. How cliché. Like some Disney film. Oh well, I didn't endow Max with the creative talent I offered Justine—poor fellow. In any case, I'll soon be—how shall I say—indisposed for a time."

Clare stepped forward. "But there's trouble coming, something called Cosmos is on the loose—"

"Yes, I've heard. Unpleasant, but then biological life is always perilous. Ask the Bhuaci, they know."

"But I can't protect Justine or anyone, not against Cosmos."

Omega laughed. "By the Divide! I never expected that. I want you to protect them from each other."

"What?"

Omega looked up as if listening to an unseen alarm. "Time's up. I must be going. Remember what I said. I saved you once; now save my family. After all, it's only fair."

In a blink of blinding light, Omega disappeared.

Clare found herself standing in the middle of a silent room. The cat meandered back onto the pillow and settled in for a contented slumber. Clare stumbled over to the edge of the bed. Her gaze slid to the multicolored giraffe in the corner. She snatched it off the floor. Tossing it on the bed, it landed peacefully next to the cat. Clare shrugged. "Go ahead; you two, sleep. I surely never will."

From Machine to Man

Originally published on The Writings of A. K. Frailey
4/21/2017

—Newearth—

"Sir? You need to wake up now, sir." The white, uniformed human shook Max's shoulder. He focused and tried to make sense of what he was seeing. A woman stood over him and peered intently into his face. Max turned away. He did not feel well. Not well at all. And wasn't that rather odd?

He closed his eyes and tried to remember. What happened? Ah, yes, Ingot thugs, mercenaries who preyed upon unwary merchants burst aboard ship and caught him just as he was transferring his data to another guard. An unlucky moment. Surely, it had been planned. But who could have known? Abanaber? He was new and seemed eager enough, but then, he disappeared once the fighting started.

Max sighed. He remembered facing the lead Ingot, a thin, sharp little being. He didn't want to have to kill him, so he raised one hand and offered—nothing. He looked down and his leg was gone. No pain. No horror. Just falling, sliding to the floor, and the Ingot standing over him, chuckling.

He blinked open his eyes.

The nurse was still there, still peering. Her brown eyes were crinkled at the edges. She was pretty, neat with short, stylishly cut hair, over fifty, and worried. Very worried.

"Sir? I need you to sit up so I can make a proper assessment. Can you do that?"

Keeping his face as neutral as possible, Max raised his upper body, expecting to list to the right since one leg was gone. But he didn't. He scowled at the end of the bed, and the outlined forms of two legs lay there in front of him. He carefully lifted the sheet that covered his lower half. Yep. Two legs. He peered up at the nurse, one eyebrow raised.

She beamed. "Yes, we managed to save it. You were nearly dead when they brought you in. Honestly, I never saw—but never mind. You pulled through, and that's all that matters, right? Now, I just need to take your vitals. You can lean back against these pillows—"

She pummeled a couple of pillows into submission and then, with a gentle shove; she pushed him back, still beaming. "There now. Feel better?"

Max opened his mouth but closed it promptly. What could he say? Did he feel better? He did not feel well. But was that better than how he had felt? How had he felt? Blinking, he realized that his head ached. He touched his head and tapped around. It did not feel like his head. It was bumpy and hard with no hair. His eyes widened as his gaze darted to the nurse's face.

She stared at an instrument panel; worry crinkles around her eyes again. "Yes, your— skull—was damaged, but we were able to replace the missing part." She glanced at him and patted his arm, a confident smile replacing the worry. "And your brain is completely intact."

Max shook his head. "I thought my leg was blown off. I had no—"

The nurse tapped a console and raised her finger for momentary silence.

Max waited.

She tapped the last time and turned to face him, offering her complete attention. "No, your leg was damaged, but it was your head that received the worst of the blast. You can thank Captain Kimberling that he got you here in time, or we may not have been able to save you. Your friend, Mr. Abanaber, has asked about you every day—for weeks."

Max bolted straight up. "Weeks? How long have I been unconscious?"

The nurse glanced at the console. "Exactly three Lunar cycles. I honestly didn't expect you to do anything this different this morning. I'm so glad you woke up. Doctor Mangham will be here momentarily." The nurse adjusted a tray near the table with studious concentration. "She wrote up a review about you for a prominent scientific journal. You're the first android she ever worked on. And such an—"

Max shook his head. "But my leg was blown off. The Captain was taken and Abanaber was nowhere to be found—"

The nurse tilted her head and smiled indulgently. "You were just dreaming. A nightmare, I'm sure. After all, it was a serious explosion. Stupid accident. Someone didn't pack their materials properly, and then you came too close with your magnetic—"

Max almost rose from the bed, but a sharp pain forced him to freeze. Holding his head in his hands, he moaned. "I can't dream. I'm an android; I—"

The nurse chuckled. "Well, maybe you *were* an android once. Not anymore. At least not completely. I saw the scans. The doctors were amazed. They wanted to do further studies, but of course, they needed your consent. It was Kelly who saved your life, really. She was the assistant on the scene. When the emergency team realized you were an android, they were going to turn you off in order to make the necessary repairs, but Kelly insisted that they check your brain functions first."

The nurse leaned in and placed a gentle hand on his shoulder. "Your android brain is overgrown with the human neurons they placed in you at creation. If they had turned you off, they would've never been able to turn you on again." She straightened up and adjusted the sheet. "You're a lucky man, Max Wheeler. Most humans add mechanical parts and turn into machines. You, on the other hand, have changed from a machine into a man. A miracle, if I may say so."

She turned to leave. "The doctor will be in shortly. Get some rest. You've awoken into a whole new life."

Max watched her leave and lay back on his pillows. He blinked and felt an odd ache behind his eyes. Apparently, being human involved some level of pain and discomfort. But then—he considered the possibilities—human?

He smiled as a tear traced its journey down his cheek.

Off-World Faith

Originally published on The Writings of A. K. Frailey
5/5/2017

—Newearth—

Bala knelt on the hard, stone floor and folded his hands across the latticed-carved railing, his head bowed. As the priest approached, he stared straight ahead; his eyes fixed on the ornate altar under the stained-glass window of Jesus embracing His Mother Mary. With precise steps, the robed figure bent and offered him a gift. The greatest gift Bala could imagine.

He accepted it, crossed himself, and stood.

When he returned to his pew, he knelt beside Kendra; her head bowed onto her hands clasped over the pew in front of her.

Final prayers and chants completed the liturgy, and Kendra sank back with a deep sigh. Her gaze floated up to the gorgeously painted ceiling.

Bala slid back on the pew and echoed her sigh. It had been so long. So much had happened. Six kids had happened. A new job, an attack on his family, and now a new threat. Bala sighed again.

Kendra reached over and clasped his hand. With a quick squeeze, she nudged him.

The procession had left, and only a few others remained behind, praying, crying, thanking God, adoring—Bala didn't know; he didn't need to know. He scooted out of the pew and Kendra followed.

Still clasping hands, they strolled through the enormous, carved doorway and stood on the top row of twenty stone steps leading into the heart of a bustling city. Saint Francis, it was called. Bala chuckled at the incongruity of the sign across the street proclaiming itself the city's finest Savings and Loan on the planet: "Saint Frances would keep his units here—if had any." Bala pointed out the sign to Kendra.

She laughed. "Well, at least they have a sense of humor, even if they have no common sense to speak of."

"Speaking of sense, I'm starving. Want to get something *before* we pick up the kids?"

"You mean to eat in peace and quiet?" Kendra's eyes widened as if she were scandalized. "What would the kids say?"

"Let's not tell them." Bala dragged her along as he led her down the street toward a fancy establishment. "Besides, I'm sure that Sister Mary Rose will have stuffed them with enough breakfast to keep them happy for at least an hour or two."

Kendra sniffed with a shrug. "If not her, then one of her fourteen sisters will see to it." Kendra halted in mid-stride. "Lord, you don't think our little darlings will end up with fifteen breakfasts, do you?"

Bala stared wide-eyed. "If they do, we'll be able to stay out for the *whole* morning." He nudged Kendra through the delicately carved glass doorway.

They followed a portly, smartly dressed waiter to a table laid with a white linen cloth and real silverware. Bala's eyes bugged. "It's been so long!"

Kendra patted his hand. "Don't go getting attached. We have to return tomorrow. This is our last fling with Old-world comforts."

Exhaling, Bala perused the menu, and they ordered two healthy breakfasts. The waiter retreated, and Kendra folded her hands in her lap. "So? What did he tell you?"

Bala tapped his water glass and frowned. "Confession is supposed to be private. You know what priests have gone through to keep—"

"Awe, come on. We always share. And besides, this was more like spiritual direction. You don't have much to confess, I imagine."

Bala shrugged. "Your imagination is lacking. Trust me, I had plenty to confess." Bala shook his head. "Funny, but when I was a kid, I used to face the priest like a soldier going into battle. I was always scared to death, shook like a leaf. This time, I felt rather sorry for the poor man. The things he must have to listen to! Felt rather sorry for myself, too."

Kendra nodded as the waiter placed two steaming cups in front of them and retreated. She returned her gaze to Bala's face. "Any conclusions?"

Bala sipped the hot coffee and blinked. "Yeah. But you won't like it. It seems that our sins make us who we are. And we forgive others and ourselves and move on, knowing all the while, we'll have to forgive again later."

Kendra sipped her coffee and then leaned across the table, clasping Bala's hand. "And?"

Bala swallowed, his gaze fixed on the tablecloth. "And I have to go. Clare will chase after Omega, but someone has to locate Cosmos. It's my duty.

I can't shrink from it, not even for you and the—" Bala swallowed back his last word.

The waiter returned with loaded trays of steaming food. He placed them silently on the table, and with a bow, retreated again.

Bala shuddered. "I have to go. If—"

Kendra squeezed his hand and nodded. "I know. Why do you think I insisted on this family trip? We needed to return to our home—to our roots. We needed to remember why we settled on Newearth in the first place."

Bala lifted his gaze and stared into Kendra's eyes. "I married you for two very good reasons."

Kendra smiled. "My charm and money?"

Bala scratched his head with a grin. "Okay, four very good reasons. But it was your wisdom and love that won me over."

Kendra picked up her fork, eyeing her food like a tiger about to pounce. "Yeah, same with me. I figured that no matter how many kids we had; you'd provide what we need. And probably not go insane in the process."

Bala chuckled and speared his ham and eggs with gusto. "Cool-headed logic, that's my middle name."

Romantic Reality

Originally published on The Writings of A. K. Frailey
5/19/2017

—Newearth—

Bala lay in bed, his arm around his wife, and stared up at the ceiling. The room glowed in soft, semi-darkness as faint starlight flowed in from the window. An abrupt snore from across the hall broke the silence. Bala chuckled. "After six of 'em, you'd think I'd get used to the idea that kids snore, but it always seems so ridiculous."

Kendra shrugged. "I don't see why they'd be any different than the rest of us. Blocked nasal passages are a part of life."

Bala squeezed Kendra's shoulder. "That's what I love about you, so romantic!"

"Just telling it as it is." She grinned. "Do you remember when we met?"

Bala stiffened. "You mean the very first time I saw you, or the first time we spoke, or the first time I kissed—"

Kendra jabbed him in the ribs. "The very first time, man-o-mine."

Bala licked his lips. "Go ahead, refresh my memory." He tickled her arm. "I know you're dying to."

Kendra rose up on one elbow and stared into Bala's eyes. "Just for that, I'll tell you what you never knew! So there!"

"Uh oh. Can I rephrase—"

"Too late, boy-o. You're going to get what you deserve." Shoving her pillows up against the headrest, she sat up and pulled the blankets straight. Her long-sleeved, purple pajamas appeared black in the dim light.

Bala heaved a sigh and curled up on his side, propping his head on his hand. "Don't mind my relaxed pose. I have to fight six children onto a transport in the morning, and I need to conserve my strength, what's left of it anyway."

Kendra kicked his foot and then positioned herself like a storyteller of old, tapping her fingers together meditatively. "I was seven—going on eight. You were nine—going on fifty." She peered down at him through the shadows. "You remember the playground at Saint Robert's? Nothing but hard cement and a few rickety swings?"

Bala nodded.

"And you trudged up the driveway with your little sack slung over your shoulder. Full of provisions, I was sure. You looked like some kind of off-world trader, come to sell his wares. I was agog with curiosity."

Bala's eyes glowed as he watched her hands gesturing. "Agog? Oh, my, you're not supposed to do that in polite society."

Kendra maintained her composure. "I didn't tell anyone, but I watched the exchange as you explained yourself to Mother Superior. You looked like a miniature soldier reporting for duty. Your family sent you with no escort, no explanation, just your provision bag, and a datapad saying that you were there for the duration."

Bala sighed. "I remember." He frowned. "How did you know?"

Kendra's grin gleamed in the half-light, which slanted across the bed. "I was very good friends with the Head Mistress. She thought the world of me. Dare say, after a few pointed questions, she told me what I wanted to know—fact wise. But I was still curious. So, I used to follow you around."

Bala slapped his forehead. "That was you? I thought that bully, MacKery, was teasing me."

"He was. I beat him up. Then I took his place."

Bala snorted, clasping his hand over his mouth to stifle any further outbursts.

"Anyway, I liked what I saw. I decided that one day you'd marry me, we'd have a family, and live on Newearth. It was my grand scheme."

Bala huffed. "Silly me. I thought I came up with the idea."

Kendra stroked the side of his face. "You would've, in fact, you did. Once I told you."

"You planned the six kids too, I suppose?"

"Hardly. They're gifts. I just hoped."

Bala nodded, raised himself to a sitting position, and folded his hands. "So, what plans do you have now?"

Kendra sighed. "That's just it. My plans only went so far. They sort of—well—life took over. I stopped planning and just tried to keep up."

Bala chuckled. "I know what you mean." He pulled Kendra into his arms. "You know, wife-o-mine. It was no accident that my bedraggled, little body showed up at that school."

Kendra tilted her head to the side, a gleam in her eye. "Oh? Really?"

Bala nodded as he shifted closer and wrapped both his arms around her, nuzzling her cheek against his. "Yep. You weren't the only one making plans. And—" Bala gazed up as though he could see through the ceiling into the impenetrable, night sky. "I don't think He's done."

Trust Me

Originally published on The Writings of A. K. Frailey
6/2/2017

—Newearth—

Eric peered through hooded, yellow eyes. His lithe, perfectly toned body stood at attention with his hands clasped serenely behind his back. He studied his boss, Simms, with absolute composure. Nothing could surprise him—he was a master of self-control and trusted no one.

Simms, a human with more replacement parts than he liked to admit, could not hide his boxy shape, though he tried. His hair, though not his own, appeared thick and black, while his olive skin tone complemented the wine-colored shirt and trousers he wore. A gold pendant hung at his neck while his bejeweled fingers flashed with color.

He sat leaning back on a well-padded chair, his feet propped up on a wide window ledge. He licked a large, chocolate-chip ice cream cone wrapped in a freeze-sleeve, which kept it nice and cold, preventing drips. Simms did not like drips. He slurped a large swipe of ice cream and then darted a glance at Eric, gesturing with his free hand. "Just say yes and make us both happy."

Eric licked his lips. "You haven't told me your plans."

Simms slammed down his feet, swerving his ice cream cone dangerously close to his desk. "What? I have to tell you everything? Who do you think I am—a beggar-boy? A Bhuac maybe?" He drew in a long breath and regained his accustomed position, swinging his feet back up on the sill. "No. You just say yes. Then I tell you my plans." He chomped down on the top of the cone and slurped his words. "Don't you trust me?"

"I already killed once for you; I think that merits some—"

"Aw, hell. You killed nobody. A nothing. What I'm talking about now is real business. My business. I have plans. Big plans." He shrugged his shoulders. "You want in or not?"

Eric straightened his already straight shoulders. "Yes."

A wide smile broke over Simms' face. He swung his feet back onto the floor and tossed his ice cream cone into the trash. "Good! Okay, let's get down to business. I'm gonna build the biggest interstellar docking bay this side of the Divide. I'm gonna—"

Eric shook his head. "Newearth already has one of the largest docking bays this side of Bothmal. You really think that—"

"Shut up, imbecile. I have already thought this through. I've Ingots, Uanyi, and even a couple dozen Crestas ready to follow my lead. I just need someone I can trust." He peered up at Eric's impassive face. "You know, killing that crossbreed was my idea. Right wasn't going to do it, but I showed her the logic of the situation, and besides, I wanted to see you in action."

"I take it, I performed to your satisfaction."

"Aw, don't talk like that, like some cheap robot off a passing trader." He clasped his hands, lacing his fingers together. "You've got to be perfectly straight with me. I need someone who'll be my eyes and ears, listen, but never talk, except to me. You get the idea? I'm gonna make Newearth the greatest trading center in the universe. And that'll make some high-profile personalities jealous. They'll try to stop me or cut in and try to replace me. And I won't stand for it!"

He waved to his wall of medals, attesting to his award-winning skill at Zinzinera, a tough, body-wrenching, head-cracking Ingoti game that many players never live to see through to the end.

"I've got the skills to make this happen. It'll be good for Newearth, good for every trader who wants to increase business, good for you, and good for me." He frowned. "There's only one person who might give me serious trouble."

Eric's eyebrows rose. "Who might that be?"

Simms heaved himself out of his chair and strode over to his wall of trophies, studying them. "A Luxonian by the name of Cerulean. He's been around a long time, since before the beginning— of Newearth, I mean. He's got a reputation as a nice guy. But he isn't. Trust me. He's as dangerous as they come." He swung around and faced Eric. "I want him outta my way."

Eric folded his arms high across his chest. "Luxonians are hard to kill."

"I didn't say *kill*. I said I want him out of my way, traveling to foreign parts, or back on Lux— whatever. But wherever he is, I want you to keep your eyes on him. I want his reputation tarnished. I want everyone to see him for what he really is."

"And what—exactly—is he?"

Simms shrugged. "He thinks he's a guardian, a protector, like some Knight of OldEarth. But it's all a lie. There are no heroes these days—they don't exist." Simms padded up to Eric and peered into his eyes. "Look into Cerulean's soul and see what you find. Then report to me. We'll find a way of destroying him—from the inside out."

Eric unfolded his arms and nodded. "Simple enough."

Simms shook his head. "Not simple. Necessary. How else will I get everyone to trust me?"

Never Forget

Originally published on The Writings of A. K. Frailey
6/16/2017

—Planet Sectine II—

Riko's home, late evening, after a surprise attack by Uanyi Extremists.

Uanyi are slim creatures with rubbery exoskeletons as well as internal bones and enormous eyes.

Riko held his mother's body in his arms, rocking silently as tears streamed down his face. Burning rocks flew to pieces, and raging flames cast his Spartan living room into eerie, violent shadows.

With his legs tucked under him, he sobbed silently. He had scrambled across the room to her when the first blast broke the west wall sending shrapnel in all directions. A section of the window frame protruded from her side.

Bending close, he pressed his ear to her chest, but no sound, no movement other than his own rocking motion signaled life. "Aw, Ma!"

—A Lunar Cycle Later—

Riko stood next to a grave mound while his sister, Rhianna, hunched next to him. A tall stone with a picture of a falling star etched in the middle perched at the head of the mound. Riko bowed his head.

Rhianna placed her arm around his shoulders. "Ma would want us to move on. It was a mistake coming here. We thought we could keep the race wars from following us, but it was a dream. We're not meant to live in Old-world Uanyi. To be honest, Old-world Uanyi wasn't so so great, even back in its glory days."

Riko lifted his head and stared at the two suns in the sky, one only a third of the size of the other. "Let's go. We don't want to be late for the transport." He peered around. "Where's Zero?"

The woman bellowed a trumpet-like call across the brown, moss-covered expanse.

A miniature Uanyi came trotting from around the side of an octagonal structure with dirt smeared across his white shirtfront, a tear in his brown leggings, and his bulbous, black, insect-like eyes wide and blinking.

The woman shook a slender finger at him. "Zero! You've been fighting again?"

Zero shook his head, his gaze as frozen as his little body.

Riko glanced at his sister. "You gotta train that kid. He'll never survive on Newearth."

The woman shrugged. "He's survived so far. Better than some." She stretched out her long, rubbery arm. "Come on, little one. You'll have to carry things for me. You'll do that won't you?"

Riko watched his sister and nephew pad away to the round-shaped house with vivid colors painted on it in a pattern unique to their family line. He shook his head.

A larger, hulking Uanyi trotted forward, waving one hand. "Hey, Riko, glad I caught you before you left." He stopped suddenly, peered sharply at the stone and the grave mound, bowed low, and then turned his attention to Riko, taking him by the arm. "You ma left you something. I had to wrestle your mother's brother for it, but I got it. Stupid fool thought that no one knew." He struggled to get something out of a deep pocket. "Your ma was a better businesswoman than most gave her credit for. Pity. She should've lived to see us transform this place—"

Riko held up his hand. "She died trying to transform this place." He heaved a sigh. "Never mind. What ya got?"

"Units. Over twenty thousand, and they're in your name." He lifted a data-chip into the air and handed it onto Riko's open palm. "Look, I know it was terrible, what happened to your ma and all, but sporadic fighting isn't the end of the world. Not this world anyway. Don't give up on us. We're trying to dig down to our roots, grow a new culture from the ancient soil of our—"

Riko stared at the chip in his palm and lifted his other hand to stall his friend. "Stop, Uncle Clem! Your brother is gone, and ma is dead. I've heard all the propaganda I ever want to. I'm done changing the world, saving our race, or whatever it is you think you're doing. I'm heading to Newearth to find work and mind my own business."

Clem glanced away. "And what about Rhianna? And Zero?"

"I'll look after them. Best as I can. Rhianna's like Ma—headstrong with good business sense. They'll be fine." He looked up and stared at the structure. "I think." He shrugged and started toward the house. "Anyway, you can always check in on us. I'll send my contact info as soon as I get to Newearth." He shoved the chip deep into his own pocket. "I appreciate everything you've done—and this." He tapped his pocket. "Few would've cared what happened to us—at least to me."

Clem threw his arm around Riko and jiggled him, friendly-like. "You saved my life once, remember? I'll never forget that."

"Yeah, well, it was luck on both our parts. Sometimes you get lucky, you know." He stopped and glanced back at the grave mound. "Sometimes—not so much."

Clem shoved Riko forward. "Better hurry. I bet you'll have zillions of units by the time I visit." He chuckled. "You better."

Riko sighed. "We'll see." He looked up at the suns. "God knows, it'll take more than units to make Newearth feel like home. Never really had a home."

Clem shrugged. "We're all trying to find our place. Your Ma wanted you to set down roots. But never forget"—he wagged a finger in Riko's face—"you're a Uanyi!"

Riko nodded and padded away, leaving his uncle and his mother's silent grave behind.

Mirage

Originally published on The Writings of A. K. Frailey
6/30/2017

—Mystery Planet—

How many years had they been married? Abbas sighed. He couldn't remember. His wife had always taken care of the details—anniversaries, birthdays, and celebrations of all kinds. He had always been too busy. *Mirage* rather than marriage demanded his unfailing obsession.

The townsfolk bowed their heads and shuffled their feet in shy obeisance as the funeral procession marched passed. His son, Omega, strode at the front helping to bear the slight weight of the petite coffin. The shoemaker, furrier, carpenter and other inhabitants marched in a stately manner to the Resting Field.

Flowers bloomed in glorious array; Abbas had made sure of that. Color splashed against the horizon from simple white daisies to blood-red roses. Though there had been murmuring among the children at the sight of spring blooms in the middle of winter, their parents had sense enough to hush the little ones and remind them that Abbas could do what other mortals could not. He was their father, after all. And today they must bury their mother.

~~~

After the intoned words of blessing upon her spirit, which everyone trusted to the outer limits of their imaginations, a wailing chant set them into mournful retreat. Abbas stood alone by the stone slab engraved with her name: *Mother*. It was her vocation and her title. Even Abbas called her 'Mother' in the intimacy of their chamber. She was, above all things, a giver of life and love.

Omega stepped to his father's side, and the two stared in silence at the grave. A red bird burst from the woods and soared into the noon sunshine. Omega lifted his tear-stained eyes and gazed in wonder. "I imagine she flew to her rest— as happy to go as to stay. She was always a cheerful being."

Abbas glanced at his son. "We grieve, nonetheless."

Omega nodded. "Yes, but perhaps we should do more. We ought to bear testimony to her spirit somehow."

Abbas shrugged and turned, his body hunched and his gaze blank. "I bore little testimony to her while she lived. I hardly—"

Omega grasped his father's long, flowing sleeve and halted him in his tracks. "But that's not true. You adored her. You fulfilled her every wish." Omega threw back his head and closed his eyes to the burning sun. "It was I who tore her heart, always racing about the universe, chasing every passing fantasy, leaving her to hug vaporous memories of my childhood and those who passed beyond."

Abbas placed a warm hand on his son's shoulder. "You were her passion. I loved her, but *Mirage* and world-making were my chosen

97

professions. It seems we three, despite our mighty powers, have been little more than star-crossed lovers."

A large, muscled man with thick, brown hair dressed in a jerkin worn over a black, cotton tunic strode forward and bowed with a hand clasped over his heart. "My lord, the townsfolk have set the repast in the main hall and await your arrival."

Abbas nodded in dignified acceptance, and the man turned to his next duty.

Omega stroked his chin with the glimmer of a smile. "Father, I have a magnificent idea! Mother enjoyed my stories of Newearth and—"

"One village is enough, son." Abbas marched at a quicker pace toward the lofty castle on the hill. His boots left no print on the rocky road.

Omega squared his shoulders as a light flared in his eyes. He hustled alongside. "She thought that the universe would be much improved if there were more places like Newearth—"

Abbas stopped suddenly. "You want to introduce other species—here? Do you realize what that would entail? The shifting of populations and the destruction of their native culture!"

Omega laughed. "But it would be a challenge. Medieval OldEarth has its limitations—as well you know. We could remake it, completely fresh, in a new century with a variety of life forms. Mother enjoyed a scene I once brought of a small farming town with a vibrant population—"

Abbas waved his hand toward the little village nestled against the hill. "And what would you do with this population? Mirage is the only world most of them have ever known."

Omega strode to the gate where an elderly woman in a long, homespun dress curtseyed in formal recognition of her Master. He clasped her wrinkled hand and gazed into her eyes. "Martha, dear, what would you say if I wanted to bring new life into this old, barren village? Would you support me?"

The old woman gazed back with devotion. "We would do anything you ask, for you are our Lord. You can do no wrong."

Omega hugged her frail shoulders and led Martha toward the open door and the lighted hall filled with tables loaded with food. "You do me great honor, my friend. And I'm sure it would please Mother. We must honor her memory with a new direction, a new life." Omega charged ahead, leaving his father on the threshold.

Abbas lifted his eyes to the sparkling, blue sky and shrugged. "He is your son as well as mine. What would you have me do?"

Mirage-Reborn

Originally published on The Writings of A. K. Frailey
7/14/2017

Like an artery, Main Street pumped life into the small town and the surrounding farms. A red, brick building sat at a jaunty angle on the southwest corner of the four-way stop. Raised letters spelled out its inception: *Mirage-Reborn Savings and Loan—Year One*. The double, front doors swung inward on well-oiled hinges into an interior meant to inspire confidence. A steel, reinforced vault behind the main counter gleamed in assurance, practically winking at you from the glinting rays of light spilling through tall, rectangular windows.

Directly across the street on the south side, a forest-green, wooden, two-story structure boasted fancy lettering: *Nelson's Grocery—Your One-Stop-Shop*. Nelson's stocked everything from fresh fruits and vegetables to floral prints for your next dressmaking project. Though old man Nelson insisted that his daughter, Grace, stock more variety, it was already almost more than she could manage. Two other Main Street stores filled in the culinary gaps—*Bud's Butcher* and a *Fresh-from-the-Farm Dairy & Bakery* outlet.

A filling station and a post office occupied the other two street corners, while the Sheriff's Office halfway down the block, ensured the current population that not only was your money safe— you were too. Or you would be soon, once Abbas introduced their new sheriff at the Town Hall meeting.

Abbas, in his ancient wisdom, had cultivated changes in Mirage slowly. It had only been in the last year that he began referring to their world as Mirage-Reborn. Clearly, the population realized that something was afoot when he replaced their medieval styled hovels with sturdier, comfier, ranch-style houses. Like a proud papa, he took each citizen—and their assembled relatives—to their new abode and showed them a thousand Oldearth years' worth of improvements in an hour. It was an accomplishment worthy of a god. The changes were accepted as divine ordinances—and darn nice ones too.

The Town Hall crowd jostled each other in friendly intimacy; after all, these people had lived together through enormous life changes. They gathered in expectation, chatting about the weather, crops, and the usual challenges of life, studiously avoiding any emphasis on the fact that their world had morphed from an Oldearth medieval village into a mid-twentieth century, American town. Would wonders never cease?

Omega had transported each of them—or their parents—to Mirage decades ago in response to a particular need. After the demise of Oldearth, Luxonians had been humanity's only hope, but occasionally, humans did not conform well to life on planet Lux. The adventurous ones struck out on their own and settled on outposts. Sometimes successfully. Sometimes disastrously. When Omega learned of a human in extreme need, he would swoop in, and, like a hero of old, save the innocent—and not so innocent—from certain destruction. Each new arrival's adjustment to medieval Oldearth society put everyone on equal footing.

After Omega's mother died, he, too, disappeared, so Abbas took up the mantle and played the combined roles of demi-god and sheriff-in-residence. Most inhabitants accepted these changes with a shrug of laconic indifference. There was nothing written in stone saying you couldn't jump a millennium or two every now and again.

Since his wife had died and Omega had left, Abbas busied himself with the town. He liked to appear suddenly, surprising the marketing crowd or lend a hand at a barn raising. He never appeared out of humor or out of breath, and he was welcomed everywhere he went.

As the crowd gathered in happy chatter, Abbas suddenly appeared in the front of the hall with two men, one on either side. On his left, a blond, slim man with striking blue eyes squared his shoulders and crossed his arms as he appeared to appraise the crowd in a critical, sweeping glance. A thicker and heavier, dark headed man on the right merely stood with his muscled arms at his side, gazing ahead like a crime suspect in a lineup.

Abbas raised his arms, and the room fell silent. "My friends, I bring you two new citizens of Mirage-Reborn. I know you will welcome them as I have welcomed you in times past." He waved to his left. "Mr. Jeremy Quinn has served many, faithful years as a Bothmal guard, but now he has agreed to serve as our Sheriff and Director of Criminal Justice."

Murmurs from the crowd stirred the air at the word *Bothmal*.

"Did he say Bothmal? As in the Inter-alien-prison?"

"Hellhole, I was told. No good can ever come of that place."

Quinn's eyes scoured the assembly, stopping at dissatisfied frowns and hovering over fear-filled eyes.

Abbas waved the murmurs away, nodded to his right, and his tight smile softened. "And here, I have brought you a treasure in Lucius Pollex, a man of renowned physical strength and the best blacksmith this side of the Divide. In him, you will discover both a hard worker and a faithful friend."

Relief warred with anxiety in the crowd's eyes as they shifted from Quinn to Pollex and back to Quinn.

"I have arranged a simple repast, so join me with our new friends at the cafe, and let's get to know each other better."

Abbas opened his arms as if in benediction, and the crowd parted with respectful nods and clasped hands. Like a wave washing over the shore, the entire population turned and followed their leader through the door.

Only Vera Webb, a petite, black-haired woman with high cheekbones, piercing black eyes, and ridges along her neck stood to the side and saw the exchange between the newcomers.

Lucius Pollex merely nodded with a hint of a warning in his eyes, but Quinn poured the malice of eons into his gaze as he glared at the blacksmith.

Vera shivered.

Mirage-Reborn
We Are LuKan

Originally published on The Writings of A. K. Frailey
7/28/2017

As a LuKan alien living in Mirage-Reborn, Vera Web stood a diminutive one and a half meters and preferred the shadows. She was naturally shy and had been taught to stay on the edges of her environment through strict cultural mores. If it had not been for the total destruction of her world by the planet-destroyer, Cosmos, she would have lived happily on her dimly lit planet LuKa for another four centuries. But as she and her brother, Pav, were on board a trader at the time of the invasion, she never had a chance to collect her things or lose her life. The trader, not knowing what else to do with two LuKan orphans, sold them.

Soon, Vera and her brother were lost in the universal struggle for survival. One that they would undoubtedly have lost. But Omega discovered them huddled in a cargo bay nearly dead from dehydration and carried them off to his world—Mirage. They were the very first non-human citizens, besides Abbas and his family, to live in his village.

To facilitate their integration, Omega transformed their neck gills into neat rills that processed the oxygenated air on the Earth-like planet. Their long, three-fingered hands and feet, he ignored, though he muted the stingers on their middle fingers so that, though they could hurt a human with a nasty shock, they could not kill on contact.

Pav took charge of farming the land Omega gave him, raising crops and fruit trees, while Vera took charge of the farm animals, mostly sheep and pigs, though they also owned three horses, five dogs, and uncounted cats. Vera also managed the farm accounts and the house.

It was soon after their initial integration that Omega disappeared. They learned his history and of his mother's death from rumors and hushed conversations on street corners, but once settled on the farm, they rarely strayed near town. Once a month, farmers came by and hauled off whatever Pav and Vera laid out for sale, be it a couple of fat sheep or three baskets of apples.

After Omega had been gone nearly a year, Vera decided to venture out and attended the Town Hall meeting in which Jeremy Quinn and Lucius Pollex were introduced. She scowled at the sight of Mr. Quinn, but something deep inside stirred at the sight of the blacksmith's somber eyes.

When Quinn showed up on her doorstep a week later, Vera knew that she should never have strayed from the farm. Pav was working on the acres farthest from the house, so she didn't even bother to scan the horizon for him.

Quinn nodded with a set smile and swept his hat off his sweaty head. "Whew! Mind if I sit on the steps for a moment? I've been traipsing around to each farm so as to introduce myself, and you're the last on today's list. I'm tired beyond words."

Vera blinked in sudden confusion. His smile caught her off guard, and his courteous tone unsettled her early assumptions. She pulled a chair forward, out of a dark corner, and gestured. "Please, make yourself comfortable. My brother is in the field, or he would meet you himself."

The sheriff's silver star pinned on his tan shirt winked in the sunlight, and he waved as if to assure her that Pav would never be missed. He plopped down in the chair with a contented sigh. "No, don't worry about Pav. I only wanted to speak with you anyway. From what I've heard, your brother is a man—I mean an alien—of few words."

Vera stiffened. Her long fingers gripped the edge of the porch railing. "We are LuKan. Shy and reclusive by nature. We do not mean to be rude."

Quinn's gaze flitted over her face, her figure, and finally to her fingers, halting for only a millisecond on the third digit with the thickened tip. "No, of course not. I'd never think the worse *of you*." He stared into her steady gaze as if to drive home a secret meaning.

Vera's grip tightened, and her gaze dropped to the ground. "Is there anything in particular that I can do for you today, Sheriff?"

Quinn wiped his brow with the back of his hand and stood. He stretched as if he had just woken from a long and comforting nap. "No, not yet." He sauntered closer and stared down at her bowed head. "I've seen a lot in my years, little Miss, and I know how things can change in a moment. It's nice to know who I can count on—if you understand."

Vera kept her eyes lowered and merely shrugged.

Contrary to his usual habit, Pav strolled out of the field in the middle of the day. He loped across the yard but said nothing. His gaze stayed fixed on the house, but his steps took him directly into Quinn's path.

Quinn replaced his hat and tapped Vera on the shoulder. "It was nice getting to know you. Let your brother know—*you're my friend*—understand?"

Vera stood frozen even as the sheriff stepped off the porch and grinned at Pav as he passed.

Pav marched up the stairs and into the house without a word. Only Vera saw his hands shaking.

When Lucius Pollex showed up on Vera's doorstep the next morning, she was not visibly surprised. Pav had gone into the fields at the first note of birdsong, so she was alone again, but this time, her shoulders didn't droop as she lowered her gaze.

The blacksmith's hair blew in a slight breeze; his hands tanned a dark brown, but his face appeared unnaturally pale. "Hello, Ma'am. Sorry to disturb you, but your brother sent word that I was to come by and fix a wagon. Would you know about that?"

Vera's gaze shot to the barn. They owned a wagon, but to the best of her knowledge, it was in perfect shape. Her brows furrowed. She led the way to the barn, pulled open the red door, and stared at a lopsided wagon with one wheel broken in half. She turned and faced the blacksmith.

"Something must have happened while he was using it the field." She dared a quick glance into Pollex's eyes. "You think you can fix it?"

Mr. Lucius Pollex glanced from the wagon to her tiny face and a warm smile gleamed from his eyes.

It was near sunset when the blacksmith showed up at her door again.

Vera stepped out into the evening light feeling rather light herself.

Mr. Pollex wiped his hands on a dirty rag and nodded. "I rolled it to my shop and worked on it, but it's going to take a bit more time. I could lend your brother a spare wagon in the meantime—if he wants it."

Vera shook her head and glanced up. She froze. Jeremy Quinn was strolling down the lane.

Mr. Pollex peered over his shoulder and closed his eyes.

Vera shifted her worried gaze from the sheriff and frowned at the blacksmith. "Are you ill?"

The blacksmith shook his head. "Not yet." He turned, and when the two men's gazes met, the sheriff smiled, waved, and strolled in another direction.

"You know each other." Vera's hands clenched behind her back.

"Yes."

"Is he your enemy?"

"I would not have it so. But he was once my jailor." The blacksmith looked up and peered into Vera's widened eyes. "Listen now. If ever you need a friend, I'll come, all right?" With a tip of his head, the blacksmith turned and strode down the lane.

When Pav came in that night, he stopped Vera on the landing before her bedroom door. He placed a gentle hand on her shoulder. "I know you are afraid, but just stay in the shadows; you'll be all right."

Vera patted her brother's arm and retreated to her room.

Later, as she wandered under the night sky and pondered her life on Mirage-Reborn, she reflected on the two men who had entered her life so unexpectedly. Her frown transformed into a soft smile as she turned from the image of the one who demanded friendship to the one who offered.

A New Life for Lucius Pollex

Originally published on The Writings of A. K. Frailey
8/11/2017

—Spaceship Alliance—

The fight was inevitable.
The outcome was not.

Sweat poured down Lucius Pollex's face as heat seared the hairs on his arms. A blast knocked him to his knees. He sucked in a lung full of air. Suddenly, a baby's wail pierced the smoke-filled corridor.

"Oh, God." Lucius' muscles gleamed as he crawled forward. He could hear Captain Akio's voice ringing in his ears. "Keep the governor safe—at all costs. She's more important than the entire force put together." Lucius shook his head and choked, nearly sobbing for air.

"Matthews! Governor Matthews! Can you hear—?"

A terrified shriek split the air.

A hologram picture of Governor Matthews signing an Inter-Alien Alliance treaty between the Friezing Outpost and the Crestonian government while cradling a newborn baby in her other arm filled his mind. The sight had left him incredulous. She was a woman of renowned diplomatic abilities, but over the year and a half he had served her, his doubt had turned to silent awe.

Lucius' shoulder grazed a corner. On his right, he heard the incessant screams of a terrified baby, on his left a blocked doorway led to the governor's private office. An explosion rocked the ship. He banged his head against the wall and struggled to stay conscious. With a fist, he pounded the closed door.

"Governor Matthews!"

The shrieks dwindled to a whimper wafting from the open doorway. Lucius turned, rose to his feet, and staggered in.

—Bothmal Prison—

Dressed in prison garb, Lucius awoke to a light beam focused on his eyes. He sat up, cupping his hands over his face as his prosthetic feet hit the cold stone floor.

"Get up. They're waiting for you."

Lucius stood and faced his jailor, a short, blond man with the name tag "Officer Quinn" imprinted on his uniform. A small man who obviously delighted in small power. *What would he do with great power?* Lucius shuddered.

Quinn jabbed Lucius' in the chest with the tip of his Dustbuster. "If you're found guilty, you're mine—forever."

Lucius shrugged. "Not forever."

"It'll feel like it before long." Quinn gestured through the doorway. "Let's go."

Lucius tripped. The lifeless prosthetics never moved as quickly as he expected. He righted himself; his gaze stayed fixed straight ahead.

~ ~ ~

In the courtroom, Lucius stood on a center dais with his hands clasped behind his back. Quinn stood near at hand, his Dustbuster at the ready. Frisian and Crestonian representatives sat in the wings.

The Crestonian judge tapped two tentacles together. "We find you guilty of gross negligence in the performance of your duty and hereby sentence you to—"

Lucius' gaze wandered from the scene and retreated to the moment he clasped the baby girl in his arms and held her tight against the searing flames. He had little memory of the rest of his rescue mission, only the moment he awoke to discover that the baby was gone and so were his feet. Why they blamed him was of little importance. They had to blame someone, and he was expendable. The Frisians and Crestonians would agree on that at least.

On the way back to his cell, Lucius stumped along in silence.

Quinn's grin appeared almost boyish. "What the hell did you expect? It's not like the baby was really worth it or anything. She's dead now, you know. Lung damage—"

Without a minuscule change in expression, Lucius reached out and gripped Quinn by the throat. He squeezed. Even when Quinn nudged the Dustbuster between them, and alarms blared throughout the corridors of Bothmal prison, Lucius kept squeezing.

—Mirage-Reborn—

Suddenly, Lucius felt a jolt sear through his body. He assumed he had just disintegrated to the tune of Quinn's Dustbuster, but to his amazement he found himself standing in a field of daisies. Lucius raised his hands and examined them. He pinched his arm. A chuckle made him turn around.

"No, you're not dead." Omega, wearing a brown jerkin and tan, cotton pants waved Lucius forward. "Nothing of the kind. Come, let's get you settled before I go."

Lucius took a tentative step forward and tripped.

Omega sighed. "Yes, sorry, I didn't fix them. Not yet, anyway. But your weakness will prove your strength." Omega smiled airily. "Right now, I just want you to rest up for new challenges. I've got a whole world waiting for you."

Lucius folded his arms across his chest and allowed his eyes to absorb the glory of a copse of woods and the flower-strewn field all around him. Slowly, his gaze wanted back to Omega. "And you are—?"

Omega sniffed and clapped his hands together. "Yes, of course. I always forget. Not everyone in the universe acknowledges me as lord and master." He stepped forward and flourished a formal bow. "I am Omega, last son of my father, a being of wisdom and dignity who will soon become like a father to you as well. He is the creator of Mirage-Reborn—your new home." Omega waved to the right, and a small, thatched cottage appeared. "But before I send you home, you need rest and time to adjust."

Lucius shook his head. "Why? I mean, why save—"

Omega strode to the cottage door and swung it wide with an even wider smile. "For the same reason I do everything. I need something from you."

Lucius stroked his chin as his eyebrows rose. "You? Need something from me?"

Omega shrugged with a tilt of his head. "You see, I must discover if the impossible is possible." His gaze delved deep into Lucius' eyes. "I am settling Quinn on Mirage-Reborn with you. I'd prefer you not kill him."

Lucius' eyes widened.

Omega waved his hand. "And he's not to kill you, of course."

A red bird burst from the grove of oaks along the edge of the woods behind the cottage and soared into the air.

Lucius caught his breath, and then let his gaze land on Omega once more. "I've already been found guilty of—"

Omega laughed. "That's why I chose you, such an honest man!" Omega gestured toward the doorway. "It is well provisioned, and you will have plenty of time to rest up. My father, Abbas, will retrieve you when he's ready. But now, I really must go. I'm terribly late." Omega raised his hand in salute.

Lucius shouted. "Wait! I don't understand—"

Omega grinned as his figure faded into the sunset; his voice carrying even after the last glimmer of his sparkling eyes disappeared. "We all have impossible choices to make."

Lucius' hands flapped to his side as he sucked in a deep, shuddering breath. He gazed at the natural beauty before him and took his first step toward home.

Grace Nelson's Murder

Originally published on The Writings of A. K. Frailey
8/25/2017

—Newearth—

I've got blood on my hands, pure and simple, but I'm not sorry. Grace Nelson pushed her father's wheelchair up a gentle incline toward a small, yellow house set aside on a winding, pave-stoned lane. *It looks like a picture on an Oldearth vintage postcard.* Grace sniffed. *So Bhuaci.* She squared her shoulders. *By the Divide, I hate it here. So blinking perfect, I could smash it.* Her eyes traveled over to a Bhuaci family strolling down the lane hand-in-hand. *Or them.*

"Grace? Why'd you stop? I'm hungry and it's getting hot." Old man Nelson swiveled his head back as far as it would go.

Grace leaned in and shoved the chair up the last steps to the brown and white front door. "Just tired, Dad. Not as young as I once was, you know."

The old man chuckled. "None of us are."

Grace turned the chair sharply about, opened the door, and started back over the threshold.

Nelson pointed a shaky finger at a Bhuac male in a trim, green uniform, brown, military-style boots, and with a severe haircut strolling toward them. "What's he want?"

Grace shuddered.

"Lawman? That you?" Nelson's wide grin accompanied his beckoning wave. "It's been some time since you wandered down this way, sir."

Lawman offered a professional smile, but his gaze swept over Grace with anxious wrinkles around his eyes. He shook the old man's hand. "It has." He cleared his throat. "Sorry to hear about your wife. I was off-planet—"

Nelson waved the concern aside. "It's better this way. She doesn't have to slave away over a decrepit, old fool anymore."

Lawman's eyes flashed to Grace again.

Grace's impenetrable stare focused on the park across the road.

Lawman gestured weakly with a pained look in his eye. "With Grace here, you'll always be well looked after."

Nelson's chuckle sounded like a cackle. "She's wasting her life on me—but I can't seem to get her to leave." His grin widened as he stared Lawman in the eye. "So, what can we help you with? Or is this a social call?"

Lawman's back straightened. "I just wanted to check in and see if I can be of service. You're our first human settlers on Helm, and I'd hate—"

Nelson's voice boomed. "Don't be ridiculous! We're not going anywhere; are we, Grace? Quite happy here. Couldn't stand Lux with that bright sun in my eyes every minute and all those high-and-mighties zipping about. Never knew when one might be in the room with you. Now, you Bhuacs may be shapeshifters, but at least you have respect for human sensibilities. You maintain your form, and nice forms they are too, quite pleasing—"

Lawman's eyes strayed over to Grace. "You're happy here, Grace?"

Grace's stiff smile matched her stony gaze. "I'm happy wherever I'm needed." She sucked in a deep breath. "And, at the moment, I am needed in the kitchen. It must be past noon."

Lawman nodded. "Certainly. Don't let me keep you. Good day." He dropped a smile on Nelson and backed away.

Grace maneuvered the wheelchair over the threshold and started to close the door.

Suddenly, Lawman gripped the edge and leaned in, peering into Grace's face. "Oh, and Grace, we know...about it." He nodded decisively. "You mustn't let it ever happen again."

An icy gleam narrowed Grace's eyes. "Don't be ridiculous." She swung her father's chair around and let the heavy door fall shut. Her shoulders hunched up near her ears as she pushed the chair into a large, well-lit kitchen with a built-in oven next to a six-foot cabinet. She parked the wheelchair next to a cushioned recliner with a small table attached on one end.

Nelson swiveled his body from the wheelchair onto the recliner and plopped down with a long sigh. He snatched a datapad from the table and began to scroll through.

Grace pulled a container from a freezer unit, popped it into the wall oven, and tapped a console. Efficiently, she laid the counter and her father's table with bowls, utensils, and linen napkins. As she poured golden liquid into sparkling, crystal glasses, her father snorted. Her head snapped up.

Nelson's eyes stayed glued to his datapad, but a smile played around his lips. "Silly fool. What does he think he's going to do? Send me back to Lux? Imprison you?"

Grace froze. Her eyes rolled over to her father. "What are you talking about?"

Nelson slapped the datapad onto his lap with one eyebrow cocked. "Oh, please. You didn't honestly think you could murder my wife without anyone noticing, did you?"

Grace reached out and leaned heavily on the counter, barely a breath escaping between her lips. "Oh, God."

Nelson waived the sentiment away. "God had little to do with it, I'm sure. Besides, I'm not angry. Frankly, the old biddy was driving me mad. I'm sure that every Bhuac this side of the Divide felt sorry for me. You know, Lawman tried to talk me out of marrying Mara. Said she was unstable." Nelson snorted. "Right about that! She may have looked like a nymph on steroids, but she acted like an Ingoti drug—"

Grace squared her shoulders and faced her father. "How long have you known?" Her blinking eyes searched the room as she wrung her hands together. "You don't think Lawman will—"

Nelson's eyes softened as he beckoned his daughter nearer. "Listen, it was my fault, really. I thought she'd liven up my final years. How was I to know she'd—"

Grace slapped the counter and swallowed; her gaze fixed on her father's side table. "I poisoned her."

"Aw, heck, she was poisoning me. Well, my sunset years, so to speak. Forget about it." Nelson picked up his datapad and tapped it. "It won't happen again. It's not like you're a serial killer or anything." He grinned and darted a glance at his daughter before returning to his pad. "Then I'd have to poison you."

Grace's cooled gaze traveled from her father's bowl to the cabinet and back to his bowl.

~~~

When Omega's shadow appeared in Grace Nelson's bedroom that night, she stifled a scream. Catching her breath, she gritted her teeth. "Lawman, is that you? Trying to scare me—"

Omega, dressed in a flowing, purple tunic with green leggings and orange slippers held up a long-fingered hand and huffed. "Hardly!" He circled the perimeter of the room. "I've been watching you, Grace Nelson, and I think you're on the brink of great self-discovery." He stroked his chin. "Or self-destruction."

Grace took a step closer, her hands balled into fists. "Who the h—?"

Omega flourished a graceful bow. "My name is Omega, last son of...oh, never mind. Listen, human, I'm trying to save your miserable life and offer you a chance. The Bhuaci are notoriously suspicious of strangers, and you certainly put their hackles up by killing one of their own, even though they admit—privately of course—that Mara's moons weren't in proper alignment—as they say."

Grace sat on the edge of her bed and rubbed her temple. "I have no idea what you're talking about."

Omega flicked his index finger upwards and a small town appeared floating in mid-air. Humans bustled in and out of markets, and cars rolled down the dusty roads.

Grace stood up, fascinated, staring at the scene. "Is that a hologram—from somewhere?"

Omega pursed his lips. "That, my dear woman, is Mirage-Reborn—your new home."

"Home? Don't be stupid. Why would I go there? It looks primitive. There's not even—"

Omega snapped his fingers and the town disappeared. "Because, Grace Nelson, if you don't go *there*, you will be murdered *here*."

Grace froze. "But my father...."

Omega laughed. "Don't worry; we'll bring him along. After all, he's the reason you need to leave. Your mother didn't die in her sleep like he says—she was very much awake—poor thing. Like father like daughter, I always say." Throwing his arm over her shoulder, he led her back to bed. "Get some sleep, Grace, and I'll arrange everything in the morning."

Grace stumbled onto her bed, pulled her covers close under her chin, closed her eyes, and wondered who she should trust—this stranger named Omega or the father she had never really known.

Vera's Wings

Originally published on The Writings of A. K. Frailey
9/8/2017

—Newearth—

Vera tossed in her sleep, her dreams disturbed by flickering flashes of light and an acrid smell that wrinkled her nose. Sweat prickled her arms and legs till she panted and threw off her covers. Suddenly, she sat bolt upright, her eyes wide and staring. Swirling smoke stung them instantly.

Flames danced and darted like flickering fingers from under the door. Skittering to the chair by her desk, she pulled on her skirt and blouse and began screaming. "Pav! Pav, where are you? Help me!"

In the echoing house, she heard only the fire crackling on the other side of the door. Gripping the handle, she pulled and then screamed as the hot metal seared her hand. Grabbing another shirt from her dresser, she wrapped her throbbing hand and darted forward. Gripping the handle again, her whole body trembled. With a snapping, click, the knob turned, the door flew open, and a rush of heat and flame knocked her backward.

In horrified amazement, Vera stared at the flames. The LuKan had a natural fear of fire. Their tender flesh burned so easily that even sunburn could cause serious health issues. Crawling backward, she scurried to the back of the room and rose to her feet, the flames flickering toward her.

"Pav?" her hand clutched at her throat. She inched over to the window and stared down. It was a six-meter drop at least. In the dark, it looked like an endless chasm.

A sound of clattering boots running up the steps made her glance at the doorway. The door had swung shut again, but now the wood was engulfed in flames. A man called through the smoke and fire.

"Vera? Are you here?"

Vera's shoulders slumped in relief. The blacksmith. "I'm here, Mr. Pollex. I can't get out, and Pav's not answering." Vera clapped her hands together and winced as the blisters made contact.

A grunt and pounding shattered the air. Mr. Pollex shouted. "Pav? Pav, can you hear me?" A splintering thwack thudded against Pav's door.

Vera closed her eyes and wiped sweat from her dripping face.

More splintering crashes and the sound of boots running across the floor. Shouts, grunts, and then silence.

Wrapping her long three-fingered hands around her middle, Vera hugged herself. She swallowed against the bile that rose in her throat and ran to the window, sucking in fresh air.

Clattering boots and heaving grunts stopped outside her door. "Vera? Vera, stand back!"

Vera pressed her back against the window frame, her shoulders shaking.

A thwack smashed through the wood door, and a sharp, red-tipped blade shone through the flames. Uncounted thrusts tore at the wood until it fell aside like a torn curtain.

Lucius Pollex stepped through the flames. His red-rimmed eyes had scoured the room before they landed on Vera huddled against the back wall. He ran to her, gripped her arm, and lifted her to her feet. "Hurry, this timber frame won't hold much longer."

She froze at the flaming doorway. Without a word, Lucius stepped behind Vera and scooped her into his arms, enfolding her little body within his, and sprang through the red and orange darts of fire. Once outside the door, he dropped her on a clear space on the landing and bent over a prone figure.

Vera gasped. "Pav!"

Before she could run over, Lucius lifted Pav's limp body over his shoulder and reached out for Vera. She shook herself, fighting nausea that bubbled up from her middle. As they descended the steps, she tripped and fell forward. Instantly, Lucius grabbed her around the waist, and, squeezing her body against his, he jogged down the last steps and through the front doorway into the smoky, night air.

Falling on her knees, Vera choked and sobbed, her hands over her face. She rocked back and forth, oblivious to everything except overwhelming pain and fear.

Shouting to her left forced her to look up. A small crowd huddled over a prone form laid out on the grass. Screaming, Vera scrambled like an injured animal toward the body. "Pav! Pav, get up. Talk to me. Pav!"

The crowd backed away.

Blinded by tears, Vera felt along Pav's body, and finally, coming to his face, she lifted herself to peer into his face. If only she could look into his eyes and make a connection.

Pav's arms were stretched out to the side, his legs lay limp and bent, his face turned up and his eyes wide open, but they saw nothing—not the stars that twinkled overhead, nor his sister's tears as they landed on his cheek.

A firm but gentle hand gripped Vera's shoulder.

She slid to the ground, her head landing on her brother's chest, sobbing, clinging with her bleeding fingers.

The hand stayed with her, gentle, undemanding, warm and real in a nightmare of searing pain.

The murmuring crowd shuffled away. Someone bent low, and a woman's voice whispered. "You want me to take her home with me? I've got room—"

Vera shivered.

Lucius tightened his grip. "Give her time. I'll watch over her tonight."

A man's voice spoke in the air above her head. "It's about out; nothing to do now but make plans to rebuild."

Lucius murmured a soft, "Tomorrow."

Footsteps padded away, voices chattering in an undertone. "Poor thing. Wonder how it started...."

Pav's body, already cold, was growing stiff.

Vera shivered, opened her eyes, and blinked at the black night, tears slipping down her blistered cheek.

An arm reached around her shoulders and carefully pulled her off her brother's body. Gently pulling her close, Lucius braced himself against a shed wall and wrapped his muscled, fire-seared and soot-coated arms around her, pressing her head to his chest.

Vera could feel his chest rising and falling and hear his heart beating in a steady rhythm. His warmth settled over her shivering frame and calmed her. She closed her eyes and let the nightmare end.

~ ~ ~

An early bird chirped in the treetops. Vera opened her eyes and stared over Lucius' charcoal-blackened shirt into a hazy world of drifting smoke, green grass, treetops, and a red sunrise.

Rising on her elbow, Vera studied the stubble-bearded face of Lucius Pollex. His warm chest still rose and fell rhythmically as she shifted her arm and looked around. Her hands stung. She stared at the red blisters on one hand and the angry red blotches over the other and her arms. Wiggling her toes, she was amazed that they didn't hurt—nothing like her hands. Her gaze drifted over Lucius. She sucked in a horrified gasp. Lucius' legs ended in smoldering stumps. "Oh, no...." Fresh tears welled in her eyes.

Lucius stirred and groaned. His eyes snapped open, and his arm squeezed protectively around Vera. When their gazes connected, he sucked in a deep breath and darted a glance around the field and burned timber. "You're alive then?"

Vera nodded. She wiped her face with the back of her hand and sat up, her eyes searching.

Pav still lay stretched out in the field. She started forward, but Lucius held her back. "Wait. I'll help." He stood and assisted her to her feet. Peering down at her thin, burned face, he shook his head. "You need care, too, or I'll be digging more than one grave this day." Rubbing a tear from her cheek, he stared down, somber, and sighed. "And that, I won't have."

Vera stared at his burned stumps; her eyes widened in horror.

Lucius pulled up a charred pant leg and revealed a metal band connecting an artificial limb to the stump of his leg. "They were burned in an accident some time ago." He raised his gaze to the blue sky and exhaled. "I was never happy about it, but now, I'm glad. If I didn't have such feet, I could never have walked across a burning floor to save you."

Lucius gaze fell over Pav's body. "Only—I wish I had wings."

Vera stepped over to her brother's body and knelt down. She lifted Pav's hand and kissed it. Looking over her shoulder, a shaky smile trembled on her lips. "The LuKan believe in the Immortal Life—today, Pav has wings for us both."

Jeremy Quinn

Originally published on The Writings of A. K. Frailey
9/22/2017

—Bothmal Prison—

Jeremy Quinn shoved his dinner tray aside and leaned back on a metal chair, a petulant scowl pressing his eyebrows into a v-formation. He glowered at the steel-gray mess hall of Bothmal prison. Rotating his jaw, he swallowed his last distasteful bite of dinner.

A man about his age, but taller and thinner, wearing the same standard blue guard uniform, ambled up and pulled out a chair opposite Quinn while balancing a dinner tray.

Quinn cleared his throat.

The thin man glanced up. "You mind?"

Quinn nudged the chair out with the toe of his steel-tipped boot, his jaw still working in a circular motion. "Not much."

Thrusting his hand out and accompanied by a stiff smile, the man leaned forward. "Name's Scott. Nice to meet you. Just started yesterday."

Quinn's eyes traveled over the angular, dark-haired man. His nose wrinkled. He could smell fear a kilometer away. "It'll feel like you've been here an eon by the end of the week."

Undeterred, Scott sat and laid out his dinner—fork on the left, knife on the right, a cup of steaming coffee upper right, salad upper left, a plate of synth-meat and vegetables front and center, fruit cup lower left, napkin unfolded neatly in his lap.

Quinn's jaw dropped as his eyes followed every precise movement of his tablemate. "By the Divide, you dining with the Luxonian Supreme Council or something?"

With a self-deprecating shrug, Scott dug into his meal with relish. He chewed slowly, carefully, his gaze surveying the room with the hint of a smile. Swallowing, he positioned himself for another foray; his gaze merely glanced off Quinn. "Pigs eat at a trough; humans should reflect their higher status."

Quinn rolled his eyes.

Two guards dropped their trays in a recycle bin that sucked everything down a shoot with a swish. They placed their hands against the print identifier, and when the door slid open, they shuffled over the threshold.

Quinn leaned forward; his elbows braced on the table. "The only difference between us and the animals locked in cages around here is the color of our uniform—and the fact that we haven't been caught yet."

Scott methodically chewed another bite, swallowed, and pointed his fork at Quinn. "Speak for yourself."

Running his fingers through his short hair, Quinn tilted his head. "You're from Lux, right?"

"Born and bred. Second generation. Though my parents have a huge OldEarth sanctuary on—"

Quinn knocked his empty cup aside. "My family was run off Lux with barely the clothes on their backs during the Crestonian Crisis. Said we were a threat to planetary security." Taking a more relaxed pose, Quinn laced his fingers behind his head. "They feared us. Humans were getting too numerous, so—"

Scott laid his fork aside and took a sip of his coffee. "Our family was large; my Uncle George has thirteen kids. In fact, they encouraged—"

"Who'd he work for?"

Scott dug into the fruit salad. "Bio-engineering Dep—"

"Oh, sure, yeah! Bio-engineers can do anything!" Quinn lowered his voice and leaned in further. "Listen, newbie, Bothmal doesn't give a—"

A red light flashed over the door accompanied by a repeated buzzing sound.

Quinn frowned and rose to his feet. "Bothmal belongs to the strongest—not the smartest." His gaze swiveled around the empty room. "You're not on Lux. Remember that."

The door slid open and a Crestonian wearing prisoner's garb hustled in. He leaned against the door, huffing, and eyed Quinn and Scott. Rotating a long metal object in two tentacles, he straightened up.

Quinn stepped to Scott's side and nudged him shoulder-to-shoulder, speaking out of the side of his mouth. "Crestonians are ingenious at fashioning weapons outta garbage. Ironic, eh?"

Scott held up his hands. "Maybe I can talk him down. He's gonna get killed if he tries anything."

Quinn's eyes gleamed. "Oh, he's dead, all right. No question about that." He shoved Scott ahead. "You talk to him. I'll be right back."

Scott glared at Quinn's retreating back, then turned and faced the prisoner, one hand sliding to his sidearm. "Listen, I'm new here, but I know every rule on record, and I want us both to get out of this room alive, okay? If you just hand over the weapon, I promise—"

The door opened, Quinn charged through, and tackled the Crestonian from behind, knocking him down. They rolled across the floor with Scott pulling out his Dustbuster, edging up and backing away, as the two opponents grappled across the room and into the airy, institutional kitchen. A wall hole labeled "Recycle Your Refuse" glowed in neon letters on the wall. Jabbing his Dustbuster under the Crestonian's chin, Quinn dragged the prisoner to the opening.

The Crestonian struggled frantically, trying to get his skewer against Quinn's midsection.

Scott dashed in and held his Dustbuster against the Crestonian's head and shouted at Quinn. "Enough! We got him."

Quinn braced himself, and with a mighty shove, he leaned the Crestonian against the hole and fired. What was left of the body was instantly suctioned into the hole.

Scott fell against the wall and stared open-mouthed at Quinn. "What the—?" He waved his Dustbuster in the air. "We had him. He knew it! We could've ended this without—"

Quinn, gulping deep breaths of air, grinned like a child winning a game. "Look at the sign, idiot."

Scott pushed off the wall, his eyes wide with fury. "He was a prisoner. He wasn't sentenced to death by the court! What gives you the right—?"

Quinn shook his head as he straightened up and swaggered back to the mess hall.

Four guards rushed in with Dustbusters at the ready. The lead man stared at Quinn. "We thought you were dead! Somehow that freak managed to cut the monitors." His eyes roved the room. "Where—?"

Quinn chuckled. "He's being recycled. More useful this way." He tucked his Dustbuster away as the other guards relaxed with relieved smiles spreading across their faces.

Scott stood with his Dustbuster dangling at his side, glaring at Quinn.

With a shrug, Quinn turned and met Scott in the middle of the room. He leaned in and whispered. "Never let an opportunity slip by." Putting an arm around Scott's shoulder, he walked him back to their table. "Since I saved your midsection, you can clean up." He patted Scott on the shoulder and then started toward the door. "Oh, and not a word. Remember, the only difference between them and us is the color of our uniform."

The door slid shut. Scott plopped down on his chair and shoved his dinner tray away.

Xavier Pax's Illusion

Originally published on The Writings of A. K. Frailey
10/20/2017

—Spaceship Summons Docked at Newearth Bay—

Luxonians—light beings that can transform into any form they wish usually matching their host's physiology.

Xavier Pax never liked to lie, but some illusions made life easier. Wearing a dark green, form-fitting bodysuit with tall brown boots, his bulky figure appeared almost trim. He tapped his short, blunt fingers on the ship's console and considered the slim, brown-eyed Luxonian before him. Cerulean was renowned throughout the region for honesty and integrity, a reputation many races found highly suspect. Still, Cerulean's plea appeared sincere, and objective evidence proved the truth of his words.

Pax folded his thick, muscular arms across his chest and lifted his chin. "So, you want me to pilot my ship with *your* chosen crew across the universe to—where—exactly?"

Wearing baggy pants and an oversized sweater, Cerulean strolled around the bridge, one hand sliding over the rail. "Omega may be powerful, but he isn't immaterial. He lives someplace." Cerulean stopped with a sigh and leaned against the captain's chair a couple of meters in front of Pax. "My sources suggest a location—" He pointed to the controls embedded in the chair. "May I?"

Pax nodded.

Cerulean tapped the console, and the starry universe on the bridge-screen suddenly refocused.

Pax's eyebrows rose. "That's quite a distance and *very* little is known about that sector. You really want to go there?"

Cerulean gripped the rail. "It's our best guess and as things stand, we had better do something fast. Cosmos is coming this way, and she's bringing her appetite."

Pax stepped forward and peered at the screen. "Which planet—?"

Cerulean started forward but stumbled.

Pax caught him under the arm. "You're not well."

Snorting back a laugh, Cerulean's gaze bounced off Pax's worried frown. "That'd be an understatement. And another reason to hurry." He jabbed a finger at a star cluster on the right. "Here, the second planet from this sun. It's presently known as Mirage—a world that Omega created for his amusement."

Pax tilted his head. "Created? A world?"

With an indulgent smile, Cerulean spread his hands wide. "Where've you been? All Newearth has been chattering about the mysterious Omega and his appearance—and disappearance—during Justine Santana's trial."

Pax crossed his arms. "The Cresta murderer?" He grinned. "Personally, I wouldn't mind being killed by something that gorgeous."

The lift door slid open, and Justine stepped forward, her gaze flickering from Cerulean to Pax and back to Cerulean. "Am I interrupting?"

Pax stepped back with a low whistle.

Cerulean beckoned Justine forward and gestured toward the screen. "Just the woman I need. Show our good captain the coordinates for Mirage."

Justine pursed her lips. "Please?"

Cerulean rolled his eyes. "Please." He cleared his throat and glanced at Pax. "She's just become a mother, so she thinks she needs to correct everyone's gram—"

"Manners." Justine's fingers flew across the console as she zoomed the screen closer to a specific star and magnified, focusing on an orbiting green planet. Slapping her hands as if to dust off the dirty work, she turned and eyed Cerulean. "Now that I am looking after my daughter's well-being, I've come to recognize the deficiencies of her environment."

Cerulean placed his hands on his hips, his voice rising in indignation. "Meaning?"

"You're the model of perfection, Cerulean, but a please and thank you every now and then won't kill you."

Pax stepped forward with a conciliatory wave. "*Please*, if you would, I'd like to be introduced."

Leaning against the railing, Cerulean gestured toward Justine. "Justine Santana—innocent human-android with visions of perfect manners—Xavier Pax—renowned ship's captain who'd like to know where the—"

Justine wiggled a warning finger. She strolled across the bridge, her gaze sweeping over every instrument panel on the bridge. "Well, equipped and state of the art. I'm impressed." She bestowed her full attention and a warm smile on Pax. "We're chasing a riddle in hopes of finding a mirage."

A light shone in Pax's eyes accompanied by a meandering, mischievous grin. He flashed a glance at Cerulean. "If you had started with that, I would have accepted immediately."

Cerulean nodded. His gaze strayed from Pax to Justine. "So glad. Now, if we can get Clare to cooperate, we'll be on our way." Cerulean started to the lift.

With a frown, Justine leaned on the railing like a woman who had no intention of moving another step. "What's your hurry? Bala and Max are already aboard the Merrimack and have signed on two good—"

With a shudder, Cerulean turned translucent, nearly disappearing from sight. He wavered and fell full length upon the deck.

In a flash, Justine bent over him, checking his vital signs.

Pax leaned forward, frowning. "I knew he was ill." He sighed and stepped back. "I guess you better take him in for healing before we begin chasing your mirages."

Cerulean opened his eyes and struggled to his feet.

Justine gripped his arm and helped him stand. Her gaze flashed to Pax. "On the contrary, we're leaving Newearth within two minutes of Clare's arrival. She's the last of our crew, and I told her to hurry." She swiveled toward the lift. "Where's Cerulean's cabin?"

Pax swallowed, marched to a console, and scrolled through room assignments. "Second level, suite five—but wait—I hardly know you—or him—or what's expected of me. How can I trust you?"

Justine's steely gaze speared Pax's wide eyes. "Same way I'm going to trust you—human who's not humane—by sheer necessity." Justine propelled Cerulean's limp form to the lift and turned, firmly grasping Cerulean's shoulder. "You think you have trust issues now, wait till you meet Clare." She tapped the door panel. "Second level."

After the door slid shut, Pax fell into the captain's chair and rubbed his temple. He snorted. "Chasing a riddle to find a mirage? Ha. I should feel right at home."

Yelsa's Choice

Originally published on The Writings of A. K. Frailey
11/3/2017

—Newearth—

Yelsa loved sunshine. The rays of light pouring down on her Elven face and perfectly petite form immersed her soul in ecstasy. She lay back on the shore, her sandaled feet falling to the side, her dark brown shorts contrasting with the tan grains of sand, while her white blouse rippled like the waves in a gentle breeze. She gazed up at a wispy cloud sweeping across the blue expanse. Birds twittered in the tree line behind her, animating a smile on her lips. "The Creator be praised—"

Her sensitive ears perked at the sound of footsteps plowing across the sand. She waited for a shadow to intercept the sun.

"Yelsa?" The voice, though deep and commanding, hinted at a need.

Raising herself on one arm, Yelsa turned and faced the being before her—a Luxonian in human form: dark skinned, muscular, black eyes, wearing casual long pants, a dark blue t-shirt, and sporting a black headscarf. Her left eyebrow arched.

"Yes? May I be of assistance, Luxonian?"

The stranger grinned as he pulled his headscarf away. "No fooling a Bhuac, is there?" Kneeling on the sand, he gazed across the waves and inhaled a cleansing breath. "Beautiful. Hard to find serenity on Newearth, but you've got something good here." Facing her, he thrust out a work-

137

roughened hand. "Roux, a friend of Cerulean. Faye gave me your name."

Yelsa sat up, shook his hand, and nodded. "Faye is revered among my people."

"Apparently she thinks a lot of you—bragged non-stop about your tracking and tactical abilities—"

Yelsa's cheeks flushed as she stood, her eyes dancing over the waves as if to find a path across. "Faye likes to exaggerate our merits—part of our culture—to always appear better than we are."

Roux heaved himself to his feet and brushed the sand from his pants. "I haven't met a race yet who wants to appear any less than the best." His sudden grin disappeared as he turned toward the woods and gestured an invitation forward.

After picking up a yellow bag, Yelsa wrapped its long, embroidered strap over her shoulder and padded across the shifting sand.

Glancing in her direction, Roux's gaze swept over her. "You've heard about Cosmos?"

Yelsa sighed. "Faye sent word through Bhuaci channels. I doubt there's anyone on Newearth who's ignorant of our impending doom."

Roux rubbed his hands across his face. "From the way most are reacting, you'd never guess. Business as usual."

"Rumor has it that Cerulean is leading a mission to find the mysterious Omega—so he can deal with her. Of course, the Inter-Alien Alliance and Newearth authorities assure us that they have everything well in hand."

The sand gave way to black earth and short grass as they entered a copse of woods. Leaning against a large, spreading oak, Roux shrugged.

"The IAA has no interest in panic, so they'll assure us of anything and everything. But the truth is.... Well, Cerulean's mission is only a part of the plan. No one, not even the Supreme Council, knows exactly where Omega lives, so the whole venture is a gamble." His gaze lingered over Yelsa as she shook the sand out her sandals, propping one hand on the tree.

Comfortable again, she crossed her arms and waited.

Roux pressed forward and strolled deeper into the park-like woods. "We're sending a ship out in search of Cosmos herself."

"To determine her exact location?" Yelsa strode along, her gaze sweeping her environment.

"To intercept and—" he hesitated and glanced her direction, "—to engage if necessary."

Furrows formed between Yelsa's blue eyes; her gaze fell to the ground as she stepped evenly at his side. "You have the IAA's authority—?"

Roux slapped his leg. "They're *lending* me a ship...." He stopped and faced her, his gaze searching hers. "Listen, I worked with Cerulean on the original Inter-Alien-Alliance, and it was no picnic, trust me. Nearly got ourselves killed. Trying to get everyone to agree is about as dangerous as waiting for Cosmos to devour us."

"So, you're taking the law—"

"We're not *taking* anything!" Roux threw back his head, closing his eyes. Inhaling a deep breath, he held up a hand. "I'm explaining this badly. Cerulean should've stopped here first. He's more eloquent."

Yelsa's chuckle brought a relieved sigh from Roux's middle.

She arched her brows. "You'll do fine. Just tell me the facts."

"Facts? Okay, the fact is that we are sending out another ship—the Merrimack—to locate Cosmos, and we need you on board."

"And if we find her, what will you do? Form a treaty—?"

Roux rolled his eyes. "A treaty like—say—Please don't eat us, or we'll be forced to cause you digestive problems?"

Yelsa stared deep into the woods. Finally, her gaze refocused, and she locked onto Roux. "Cosmos devoured our sister planet. My sister lived there...."

Roux closed his eyes; his hand pressed together. After a moment, he blew air between his lips and glanced at Yelsa. "You understand why we need you."

Yelsa took the lead and marched along the winding path, slapping stray vines out of her way. After hiking a steep hill, she stopped at the edge of a vast viewing platform overlooking Newearth's largest transport docking bay. "Once you direct me to the Merrimack's shuttle, I'll know exactly what to do."

Jazzmarie

Originally published on The Writings of A. K. Frailey
11/17/2017

—Spaceship Merrimack—

The grin on Jazzmarie's face startled Max. As an android with human tendencies, or, as Cerulean like to say—*Android Extraordinaire*—Max considered himself something of an expert on pretty much everything. But from the moment that Jazzmarie first stepped her dainty foot on the deck of the Merrimack, he felt bewildered. Worse—completely disarmed. He glanced over as she tapped the communications console. She was still grinning. Max veered his eyes away. Quickly.

Jazzmarie looked up and stared, her grin still wavering like a mirage in the desert. "By the Divide, what are you so scared of?"

Though Max's skin was entirely synthetic and he could never actually jump out of it, suddenly the Oldearth expression made horrific sense to him. Clamping his jaws into what he hoped were impressive bulges, he turned sharply. "I am not scared of anything." His gaze skimmed directly over Jazzmarie's head.

Stepping over, Jazzmarie propped herself on her tiptoes and raised her head to eye level, intercepting his gaze. "So why do you look pale enough to rival a Greek Goddess?"

Flummoxed, Max's eyes searched for an escape. His gaze grazed her lips. "For your information, Miss Marie—"

"Nope."

Max tilted his head; his mouth froze in the O position.

"My name is *Jazzmarie*. One word. My parents liked how the sounds flowed together." Her fingers caressed the edge of the console as she emitted a plaintive sigh. "I wouldn't have minded something from my native Oldearth heritage like Arjun or Sachin, but—" the grin was swallowed whole by a determined pout, "—Mom liked Jazz and Dad liked Marie, so...."

With a blank stare, Max reverted to the facts at hand. "I'm not scared—just naturally pale. I am an android embedded with an embryonic human brain that has developed—actually overwhelmed—parts of me."

Raising one eyebrow, Jazzmarie twirled toward the medical database console and tapped the surface. "Which parts?"

Max practiced an eye roll like the one he had seen Cerulean preform to devastating effect. Unfortunately, it took three tries to achieve a complete rotation. Max gripped the railing for support.

Jazzmarie waved with a couple dainty fingers. "Just joking. I know all about you. Don't think I would sign aboard a mission without knowing the crew intimately—do you?" With a startling jerk, she stretched and yawned. "By golly, I've already put in a full day. What say we get something to eat? This little rocket ship has got a sweet canteen according to the specs."

Max squared his shoulders and lifted his head. If he was right, this formidable woman had just asked him for a date. Flinging a gallant elbow aside, he nodded his assent.

Jazzmarie took his arm; her grin led the way.

~~~

The canteen's décor left much to be desired by most human standards. Gray walls surrounding three, pale blue tables with seats enough for twelve, and the barest culinary choices set a Spartan tone. Max ordered his favorite yogurt-plus and a coffee, while Jazzmarie selected a grilled tomato and cheese sandwich and a hot cocoa.

Jazzmarie slipped onto one swivel chair, sliding her tray on the table, and huffed in disgust. "Good thing I have a vivid imagination or this wasteland would get me down." She snapped her fingers in Max's direction. "Wait—great idea flooding my brain!"

Horror rippled across Max's face as he spluttered his coffee.

Without ceremony, Jazzmarie mopped up the spray. "I have a set of OldEarth visuals that I can plaster over the walls. It'll look so cool—"

Max attempted a semblance of dignity. "Our preferred temperature range is—"

"Just an ancient expression, Maximan. Now, look—" She sipped hot cocoa from her mug. "I've researched everything about this Cosmos we're chasing, but I bet you know more. You've traveled all the highways and byways—right? I want to see this mission from your perspective."

Holding a spoon brimful of a yogurt-granola mix approximately seventeen centimeters from his open mouth, Max waited.

Jazzmarie frowned. "What?"

Resuming his trajectory, Max slurped, chewed, and swallowed. He tilted his head in consideration of the woman across the table. "I do not think it is within the realm of possibility that you see anything from my perspective. It isn't physically—"

Jazzmarie waved his words away like dust. "So? You think we can stop this monster?"

Placing his spoon beside his bowl, Max crossed his legs and leaned back. He attempted a studious expression. "I must take issue with the term 'monster.' Technically, Cosmos is a massive, simple-celled, space creature that feeds off planetary matter. While a monster is—"

"Someone's nightmare, I know." Jazzmarie's gaze traveled around the perimeter of the room. "She's got that painted all over her." Jazzmarie's gaze returned to Max. She let it rove over him a moment as a slow smile tugged at her lips. "I like your style, Maximan. No jumping to conclusions or hasty appraisals." She took a huge bite out of her sandwich and chewed, her grin back in full force.

Max gulped his coffee heedless of the burn scorching his throat.

After Jazzmarie had polished off her sandwich and pushed aside her empty cup, she snatched a glance at her data-pad. "Jumping Jackdogs, Roux and the new gal will be here any moment." She pointed to the pink, gelatinous mass in front of him. "You better finish that up in a hurry, or you might look unprofessional on your first day."

Grabbing the edge of the dish, Max lifted it to his lips and slurped the contents in one last, desperate effort.

The door slid open, revealing the Luxonian commanding officer, Roux, and his Bhuaci assistant, Yelsa Prater, standing side-by-side. Roux stepped in, and Yelsa followed.

Jazzmarie shot to her feet saluting smartly.

Roux walked forward; a little frown embedded in his forehead. "No ceremony with me, Doctor." He glanced at Max.

Max stood and thrust out a stiff hand. A pink circle highlighted his lips.

Roux's hand rose to his face with an automatic swiping motion. Regaining his composure, he shook Max's hand, sparing a hesitant glance at the doctor. "Max, you and the doctor have gotten acquainted, I see." After a sizable swallow, he faced the doctor head-on. "Are you comfortably settled in?"

With the most serious expression Max had seen all day, Jazzmarie nodded and clipped her words with deadly precision. "Certainly. Thank you for asking." Her gaze fixed on Yelsa. "I've been looking forward to meeting you."

Roux waved in Yelsa's direction. "Yelsa Prater, tactical expert, the renowned Doctor Jazzmarie."

Yelsa swung out a confident hand. "It is an honor. *I* have been looking forward to meeting *you*."

Roux's gaze swept over Max who stood back watching with raised eyebrows, the pink circle still in place. As a sweat broke over his brow,

Roux gripped Max's arm. "I need to see you a moment." With an authoritative tug, he jerked Max to the other side of the room, swiped a napkin from a dispenser, and waved it in the direction of Max's mouth.

In bug-eyed comprehension, Max wiped his lips. "Sorry, sir. I was distracted—"

Roux shook his head and glanced back at the two women. "Never mind." His gaze stayed fixed on the doctor. After a moment, he turned and faced Max. "I'm just glad that Doctor Jazzmarie didn't see your...little indiscretion."

Max shrugged. "She practically choreographed—" He blinked. "Why do you say that?"

With another tug, Roux yanked Max to a side counter and turned his back on the women. "You're not from around here, so you wouldn't know her reputation. Just don't make that woman mad; that's all I ask. She is Newearth's medical leader in alien biology and has more reconstruction surgeries under her belt than any being this side of the Divide, but her temper is as renowned as she is—devilish—they say."

Tilting his body slightly, Max veered his gaze around Roux and over the renowned, and now quite composed, Doctor Jazzmarie. Taking a deep breath, he nodded and swiveled back to Roux. "She certainly has a dangerous grin."

Riko's Uncle Clem

Originally published on The Writings of A. K. Frailey
12/1/2017

Uanyi are small, slim creatures, standing about four to five feet tall. They are insectine with soft, rubbery exoskeletons as well as internal bones. Uanyi most prominent features are their enormous eyes, some almost a foot in diameter, which is endearing to some, but nightmare fuel to others. Their bright colorations are also striking as are their long necks. Uanyi do not breathe the same air mixture as humans, and so they wear breathing masks that cover their mouths. Many humans find their crab-like mandibles rather frightening. Although they speak with synthesized voices, they have a terrific grasp of various languages.

Ingoti are large, ranging from six to seven feet tall. They are heavy due to their extensive weight and girth but are fast and extremely powerful. They are never seen outside of their bulky techno-organic armor and breather helms, leading some to believe that they are in fact cyborgs and that the "armor" is built directly into their bodies. They are scientists at heart, but their moral reasoning tends to be very black-and-white, almost child-like.

—Newearth—

Riko stared at the larger-than-life screen and felt his Uanyi physique tremble beneath his immaculate white shirt and pressed, dark blue pants. He swallowed and tried not to blink too rapidly.

Uncle Clem beamed a radiant grin across the universe, his excitement apparent in his waving hands and nearly epileptic shaking. "It'll be like ol' times, Riko! You and me—against all opposing forces. We can—"

Riko raised a thick-fingered hand. "Uncle Clem, stop! Listen. It's not like that here. I own an establishment, a nice place. Beings come from all over Newearth just to enjoy my varied cuisine and OldEarth-style comforts. There are *no* opposing forces."

With a shake of his head, Uncle Clem dispelled that foolish naiveté. "If you think that just because things are calm at the moment means it'll always be so, then you're not thinking like a Uanyi. We know our history. Worlds change. Cultures change. Clashes are inevitable."

A clattering of dishes falling into the auto wash forced Riko to glance away and yell at the new waiter. "Hey, careful there! Dents ruin reputations. You're not paid to kill my business."

Apologetic murmurs and a softer rattling allowed Riko to return to his uncle. "Listen, you're welcome to come and stay as long as you like. I just don't want you to think that you need to fix anything. Nothing is broken. Life is good here."

Uncle Clem nodded, his shoulders straighter and his eyes darker. "You do know about Cosmos, the planet-eater, right?"

Riko swallowed, his hands clasped behind his back. "I've heard rumors—but they're only rumors. I've got friends, and they're looking into things. The Inter-alien Alliance is working with the Luxonian Supreme Council, and even the Ingoti Magisterium is—"

A weary hand stopped Riko's assurances. "And the humans? What about the Newearth Governor? She's gonna let alien races decide Newearth's fate?"

A huge Ingot strode forward in her bulky techno-organic armor and hissed through her breathing helm in Riko's ear.

Riko scrunched his shoulders reflexively. He listened and then glanced back at the screen. "Listen, I got to get back to work. One of my customers just drank himself under the table, and no one wants to admit that he's got a problem. A regular...you know." Riko heaved his shoulders and shook off his concerns. "I'm glad you're coming, Uncle Clem, really. Just don't expect too much. We live a pretty boring existence here—and I don't want to change that. You understand?"

Uncle Clem held up his laced, tented fingers in Uanyi *I-promise-or-hope-to-die* fashion. "Trust me. I want what you want. I'm just coming to see you and bask in your success."

Riko nodded. "Stupendous. See you in the next moon cycle then."

The screen blinked to black, and Riko stood silent.

The Ingot returned and tapped him on the shoulder.

Riko looked up, his huge bulbous eyes fixed on his hostess. "Yeah? What now?"

The ingot shrugged sheepishly. "Taking a bit of risk—aren't you?"

Riko glared and poked the Ingot in the chest. "What's the risk? He'll come, and everything'll be fine."

"Maybe. Or he'll come and find nothing but space debris." The Ingot paced away. "Course, he could get in the way and *become* space debris."

Riko froze.

Common Destiny

Originally published on The Writings of A. K. Frailey
12/15/2017

Luxonians—light beings from planet Lux that can transform into any form they wish, usually matching their host's physiology.

Crestonians—amphibious beings from the planet Crestar. They have no bones and wear a mechanical exoskeleton when out of the water. They have long, soft bodies and tentacles, while their eyes are large and watery. A large "brain sack" is tucked in a spiral shell on their head.

Ingoti—androids from the planet Ingilium are large beings—up to seven feet tall with extensive weight and girth but still fast and powerful. They are never seen outside of their techno-organic armor and breather helms.

Bhuaci—shapeshifters from the planet Helm are gelatinous beings and often called the "perfect race" as they mold themselves into the physical ideal of any race they encounter. They have suffered massive persecution, and their sister planet was destroyed by the planet-eater Cosmos.

—Newearth—

Cerulean, in his human form, wore casual clothes and stared at the magnificent painting before him—his gaze absorbing the hues of the

151

landscape and the textures of the OldEarth farmhouse like a dying man inhaling his last, wholesome breath. Though the airy space surrounding him framed a myriad of OldEarth masterpieces in pristine clarity, a weary, echoing silence hung in the air.

Supreme Judge Sterling, a tall, ascetic-looking Luxonian arrayed in long, formal robes with flowing sleeves, strolled across the art gallery and stood shoulder-to-shoulder with Cerulean—kindred spirits with vastly different points of view.

Before either acknowledged the other, slapping footsteps drew near, rhythmically pacing the distance across the highly polished floor.

A Crestonian, Taug, in high, thick boots eyed the two Luxonians. He stopped two meters away. His bulbous eyes followed the zigzagging path of a horsefly, which suddenly alighted on a bench and morphed into a lithe, almond-eyed, young woman. The Crestonian exchanged grins with the Bhuaci female—Faye.

Sterling lifted his arm in salute. "Welcome, Taug, Faye! We're glad you were able to come. We are still expecting Riko—"

A Uanyi in a crisp, white shirt, tight, blue slacks and wearing an OldEarth ball cap clumped into the room, his gaze swung right and left in long, sweeping arcs. As he met Cerulean's gaze, he slowed and tilted his head in inquiry.

Refusing any delay, Sterling ushered them into a right corridor where the light dimmed to a faint glow. Landscape paintings of ancient OldEarth monuments arrayed the walls in somber reminiscence.

The passage flowed into a smaller, mustard-yellow room simply furnished with a circular table, chairs, and a counter armed with assorted drinks. With a snap of his fingers, Sterling illuminated a brilliant hologram of Newearth turning in space. Docked at one of the three modest satellite stations off Newearth, a small, red ship glowed in readiness.

After clearing his throat, Sterling's deep timbered voice broke the expectant silence. "My friends, may I introduce—The Summons. She awaits her crew—ready for her glorious mission—to chase a riddle and ensure our salvation."

Taug's bulbous eyes flickered from Sterling to Cerulean, one tentacle rose. "Translation?"

Darting a glance at Sterling, Cerulean stepped forward. "I'm leading a small crew to the Divide to find Omega in the hopes that he will help us to defeat Cosmos before she arrives."

Faye's naturally pale face, blanched to sheer whiteness. "You go to your death. *No one* goes to the Divide."

Taug flicked a tentacle airily. "Well, some go in, but none come out."

Sterling strolled around the hovering hologram and pointed to a black mass. "It's true; the Divide is a vast mystery leading unwary ships to their demise, but in our own desperation, Luxonians investigated further than any other beings, and we have found it is possible to get very close, jumping from safe space to another, like jumping from stone to stone across an ocean."

Riko plodded forward, staring at the black mass. "Fool's errand." His wide-eyed gaze lifted and surveyed the assembly with a slight shrug. "Of course, since death is imminent anyway—"

Cerulean clapped his hands in impatience. "We have no choice. *I* have no choice, and I'm leading a willing crew. No one is forced to come. But while I search out Omega, there will be another ship—"

Sterling snapped his fingers again and another spacecraft—smaller, more angular, and metallic gray—floated at docking bay two, next to the Summons. "The Merrimack—a marvel of modern engineering—is ready to search out our common enemy and monitor her every movement."

Riko's glare zeroed in on the small craft. "With all our abilities, one of our races should have destroyed Cosmos generations ago. Why is it left to Newearth to defeat her now?"

Touring around the hologram, Cerulean's fingers slid along the table edge. He stopped in front of Riko and stared down. "Because no one dared. She is a planet-eating terror, and she always strikes the weakest planets. Like a virus, she smells discord and pounces when the inhabitants are obsessed with turmoil." He sighed and moved past Riko, circling around, his gaze flowing over Newearth, absorbing her marble-like beauty.

"Newearth has been ripe for a disaster since her inception, but we have been gaining strength of late. We're at a crossroads, whether to sink into a morass of divided beings or grow into a stronger world, ready to embrace a universe of possibilities. Cosmos knows this. She has waited for this ripening and now turns her appetite toward us."

"We're doomed?" Faye's child-like eyes brimmed with tears.

Placing a firm hand on Cerulean's shoulder, Sterling surveyed the assembly. "Not—if you save yourselves."

Cerulean opened his arms. "This is Newearth's hour of Common Destiny. What shall it be? An ancient death, devoured by an unfeeling beast or rising to new life?"

Taug nodded to the floor, then raised his bulbous eyes and grinned. "I'd like to stay alive. Where would you have me serve?"

Cerulean's gaze flickered over Faye.

Grabbing Taug's tentacle, she stepped up to Cerulean. "We'll serve together."

Four pairs of eyes swiveled toward Riko.

Riko pursed his lips and rubbed his jaw. "Yeah, yeah. You'll need a communication center on Newearth, and my café serves up the wildest gossip possible—this side of the Divide—right along with our quality food."

Sterling grinned. "Common Destiny prevails."

Now I See

Originally published on The Writings of A. K. Frailey
1/12/2018

—OldEarth—

A longhaired, square-shouldered man with a thin scar under his eye, wearing a short leather tunic and fibrous sandals, paced toward a rough cave entrance at the top of a steep rise. Gripping a carved walking stick in his hand, he pounded it against the rocky ground with each step.

A barefoot, slender woman with a pile of black hair coiled atop her head, wearing a thick, woolen tunic traipsed along behind. Tripping on a sharp stone, she yelped and reached out.

The man spun about and grabbed her hand. "Itali!" With a snort of caution, he nodded to her feet. "Careful. It gets rougher."

Itali cupped his hand in hers and let him pull her closer, directing her to a smoother path. "Etum?"

Pulling her along the rise, he studied their path. "What?"

"Am I the first?"

Halting in mid-stride, Etum stopped and turned. Caressing her soft cheek, he grinned. "No one but you."

Smiling from ear-to-ear, Itali dropped his hand and raced up the last steps to the cave entrance. With a rosy blush, she charged in.

A dark shadow falling across his face, Etum trotted after her and entered the cave.

The darkness beat the light of day to the edge of the cave entrance. A musty smell and a pile of leaves alerted Itali to the cold fireplace. Squatting, she stacked dry leaves with a practiced hand and laid twigs with strategic skill.

Etum knelt to her right and worked the flint, raising sparks, which soon kindled an infant fire. As the flames grew stronger, he trotted deeper into the cave and bundled broken branches into his arms. Laying three pieces in tripod fashion over the fire, he sniffed in satisfaction.

Itali caught his gaze and grinned in daring merriment. "Now?"

With a nod, he stood and clasped her hand. They turned and stepped to the right, facing a smooth wall. The flickering firelight illuminated a painting depicting a man with a spear before a large, horned animal. Itali gasped, sending a grin bounding across Etum's features. Etum clasped his hands behind his back, his chest thrust forward and his chin rose. "You like it?"

In rapture, Itali clutched his arm and squeezed. "It's beautiful. The best yet."

Holding her close, Etum pointed to the place directly behind the painted man. "I'll add you in if you'd like."

Tilting her head, she scowled. "But how will anyone know it is you—or me?"

"I'll tell them."

"But when you're not here. In the time to come?"

Etum considered the painting through brooding eyes.

Lifting a soft finger, Itali traced the scar on his face. Suddenly, she spun around, grabbed a stick from the fire, and knocked the flame dead, leaving only a sharp, smoldering tip. She handed it to him.

Etum frowned. "With this?"

"Draw—so all will know the master's sign." She pointed to a blank space near the man.

Leaning in concentration, Etum pressed the blackened stick against the cave wall, drew a face and seared it with a double wedge on the left side.

Itali took the stick and gestured to her hair. "When you draw me, add this, so all will know it is me." She turned the stick so the wedge formed a peak at the top.

As the fire grew, so the gleam in Etum's eyes brightened. "Now—I see."

—Planet Lux—

Teal, a Luxonian light being in the form of a tall, angular, middle-aged man with thinning blond hair strode through his bedroom doorway and laughed at his wife. "You're in bed already?" Plunking down on the edge of a curved couch, he clasped his hands together and sighed.

Violet, shimmering in her Luxonian light form as a lavender Bhuaci beauty with striking almond-shaped eyes beckoned with one finger. "You look terrible. Why didn't you come home earlier? You know how exhausted you get with them."

With a shrug, Teal shook his head. "I couldn't leave. You'll never believe what my artistic couple has discovered."

Smoothing back the silky sheets, Violet rose and prowled to Teal's side. Sliding herself under his arm, she snuggled in close. "You're right; I'll never guess. So, tell me."

Teal leaned back, pulling her tight against his chest. "Writing. They caught onto the idea. A signature today—tomorrow—who knows?" He ran his fingers through her sumptuous hair, smoothing it under his chin. "You smell delicious."

Violet arched one raven eyebrow and tapped a scar along his chin. "Well, at least you've healed up. Those blasted barbarian—"

Kissing her palm, Teal chuckled. "It was an accident. They meant no harm. I approached too quickly and scared them." Lying back again, his gaze rose toward the round ceiling window studded with brilliant stars and the glow of three moons. He sucked in a deep, cleansing breath. "They have remarkable qualities. No telling what they'll learn—in a few thousand years." His gaze met Violet's. "I'm recommending to the Supreme Council that we continue our observations. I believe that this species has great potential; someday they may even be in a position to help us."

Violet lowered herself onto Teal, purring as she slid snugly into place. "That's why I love you so much. You always see the best in others—even humans."

Out Last the Ages

Originally published on The Writings of A. K. Frailey
2/9/2018

—OldEarth—

Ancient Egypt

Atet stood by the small open grave, staring upon the face of her son. Ma'nakhtuf's body lay crushed and broken, though his face remained unscathed by the falling stone. Only the frozen grimace of final anguish told the full tale. A sculptor by trade, but a dutiful son by heart, he had the gift of beauty in both body and soul.

Turning away, Atet faced the setting sun. The Pyramid's glory shown more distinctly as the golden rays of the gods caressed its edges. For this, her son had lived, and for this, he had died.

The slender figure of her sister, Khumit, wrapped in a long dress, swayed across the cooling evening sands and approached with hands outstretched. No words needed, they embraced, and Khumit clung with devotion born of mutual suffering.

Pulling back, Khumit plumbed the depths of Atet's despairing eyes. "They will come and set him to rest. His spirit—"

Atet jerked away; her eyes barren of dreams, her soul dead to hope. "The gods live on; the pharaohs live on; the glorious and the wealthy live on, but my son is dead to this world and to the next."

With a swift wave, Khumit encompassed the mighty structure. "His work lives in the pyramid, the home of the gods. All who served faithfully will outlast the ages."

A procession of men, women, and children wound serpentine fashion across the sands toward the gravesite. Clouds of incense floated before them, rising like an evening oblation.

Khumit gripped her sister's arm and drew her back to the graveside. "It is time to say goodbye; allow your son to find a new abode."

Atet stared at the grimaced face of her dead child, and like the incense floating aloft, she offered a prayer. *What I see with my eyes destroys all joy, but what I hope with my heart offers my only strength. May you live on, my son, and take your beauty with you."*

—Commander Rumson of Crestar—

Reporting on the Third Planet—District 48.78

There have been few significant changes since my last report, though I have seen Luxonian activity in the area. I also passed an Ingoti trader in close proximity. We're not the only ones keeping an eye on this planet.

One point of interest—a new pyramid structure is now set in a vast desert. I came in for a better view and have attached the measurements and significant data. This is a surprising achievement considering their lack of tools. Circling above, I could detect no discernable purpose for the structure. Interested, I ventured closer for a more intimate view and discovered a funeral procession in progress. As I observed superstitious traditions typical of this species and of no particular value to us, I ended my tour.

My current analysis for the Crestonian Science Department—as a race obsessed with structures, humans make exceptional use of tools. Devotion to their dead, though motivational to some, remains useless to us. Perhaps, given time, they will join passion with purpose and develop something we can value. Until then, I recommend we maintain regular observation but take no further action. After all, their pyramids may last longer than they do.

The Great Wall

Originally published on The Writings of A. K. Frailey
3/23/2018

—OldEarth—

Jian never liked heights, but as the head workman in charge of this section of the Great Wall, he ignored his personal inclinations. Duty ruled his will. He managed seventy slaves in turn. What they did with their wills was of little consequence—as long as they obeyed him, and he lived to see another day.

His gaze roved across the incoming bank of clouds. The wind sent his thin, dark clothes rippling like a banner on a high tower. He sniffed. The scent of rain permeated the air. Biting his lip, he marched along the outer edge of the western bank. A solid wall of earth rose in a sharp incline. Amazing what desperate men could do when enough pressure was applied.

His stomach rumbled as his gaze flickered back to the sky. The sun, obliterated by thick clouds, still offered enough light to see clearly. A fierce gust blasted across the valley nearly tottering the men on the top edge. As the strongest struggled for balance, an old man staggered and fell to his knees.

With a commanding frown, Jian marched over and stared the slave back onto his feet. The old man's shaking limbs refused the order.

"What's wrong with you, old one?"

A young man, thin to the point of emaciation with a mop of black hair, stepped forward, swiping a rag from his head and bowing from the waist. "He's ill. He needs rest or the wind will carry him off."

Jian rubbed his chin as his gaze swept from the watching assembly to the rising cloud. "A storm is coming. It'll stop work—for a week maybe."

The young man nodded. "When we start again, you will have all your workers. Or one less— maybe."

A glinting smile acknowledged the clear logic. With a quick thrust, he jerked his hand in the air and barked his order. "Clear out before the storm."

With haste and relieved chattering, the men gathered baskets and tools and began a straggled march back to camp. The old man, assisted by the young man, began to limp down the incline.

Jian halted the assistant. "What is your name, audacious one?"

The young man froze; his gaze fixed on the ground. "Hung."

The glint reincarnated into a challenge. "The name means courageous—are you?"

Hung slid a glance to the old man and released his grip. Another man stepped forward and took Hung's place, helping the ancient along. The two hobbled away.

Jian's searing gaze narrowed on Hung.

His head bowed, Hung remained calm, like a pond on a still night.

"Speak!"

Hung lifted his face a fraction. "My mother always said—it is not the name that makes the man but the man that makes the name."

"Slaves are like insects—they live but a brief season."

Raindrops splattered on Hung's face, the driving wind hurling its fury against him.

"Insects have no names. And no will of their own."

Jian crossed his muscled arm over his chest, ignoring the swirling tempest growing in his midst. "*Slaves* live to obey their masters."

Hung's shoulders hunched lower; his head dropped like a battering ram against the wind. His words, driven by the wind, raced like a message from one elemental force to another. "Who do masters obey?"

With a lifted hand, Jian took one enraged step. And slipped. The conquering wind carried him down the mud-slick incline.

Never raising his eyes, Hung plowed through the soaking rain, following the course he had traveled every day for years.

—Planet Helm—

Rosella tapped her stylus against her lips. The Bhuaci classroom, empty now, except for a cooing pair of turtledoves that perched on the windowsill, echoed the faint sound of chattering children just released from a long day of Alien-Life Studies.

Rosella closed her eyes and laid the stylus on her datapad.

"Stealing a little peace and quiet?" The most handsome Bhuaci this side of the Divide sauntered into the room, twirled the teacher's chair ninety degrees, and leaned in, his gaze not ten centimeters from Rosella's blinking eyes.

"Not stealing." She leaned just out of reach. "Just thinking." Her gaze roved over the male in front of her. "What do you want, Lutein? Here to say goodbye before you head off-world on another intriguing adventure?"

Lutein's bright eyes dimmed as he slammed a fisted hand against his chest. "I'm staggered! Just stab me in the heart why don't you?"

Rosella's eyes widened in mock confusion. "I— stab *your* heart? I'd much rather cut it out—if I could find it. At least then, it might feed the wildlife and serve some noble purpose."

Dropping his head to his chest, Lutein's shoulders drooped in melancholy grief. "I just returned from an intriguing adventure. One I was going to share with you." His gaze peeked up. "But now—"

With a weary shake of her head, Rosella nodded to the edge of the desk. "Be quick. I have to come up with a scintillating lesson tomorrow, or my students will revolt and feed me to the doves." She flicked a finger at the cooing specimens of purity and innocence.

Perching on the desk, Lutein rubbed his jaw. "Your mind has taken a dark turn since I left. Now let me see if I can brighten your spirits. Later, I'll feed you something besides my heart." He grinned. "Maybe."

Rosella's face remained impassive; her hands clasped.

"You see, I observed the newest find—the ones Song calls humans. I toured a beautiful green

166

land where the inhabitants build an enormous wall—to keep invaders out."

Rosella's chin jutted forward. "There are many walls, Lutein. Everyone has one."

"Ay! That's just what I discovered. You see; I saw another wall, but this one was inside a man, a wall that poverty and injustice could not climb over or break down."

Rosella leaned closer, her eyes widening. "You saw—"

"A wall built—of a man's will. A wall like none other."

Rosella stood and stepped near, peering deep into Lutein's eyes. "Are you the same Bhuaci that left me crying on the beach?"

Lutein stood and bowed his head; his hands hung limply at his side. "I am—and I am not."

Rosella turned away, covering her face with her hands. "That's no answer."

Lutein lifted his head. "You're right not to trust me. But—" He strode over to the wall map and pointed to a distant star cluster. "I've learned that a man who holds his head too high is likely to fall off his feet."

A sneer curled around Rosella's lips. "Your head has ever been held high, Lutein. It is one of your greatest charms. And most deceiving lies."

"So, I have learned." Grasping Rosella's hand, he led her back to her chair. "The man with the unbreakable wall kept on his feet by bowing his head."

"Can you learn to bow your head, Lutein?"

Peering at the star cluster, Lutein's gaze roamed over a vast distance. "The man with the unbreakable will loved an old man—" He swiveled around and stared at the schoolteacher. "If the will obeys the heart—it holds true—even when it is bowed."

A smile—like the morning sun—broke over Rosella's face.

Live

Originally published on The Writings of A. K. Frailey
4/6/2018

—OldEarth—

Daud leaned upon his shepherd's staff and tipped back his head. A brilliant star lit the night sky in a thousand points of light. Heart-pounding exuberance flushed his face as he stared at this new, unfathomable mystery. His brother, Hikmat, teased him unmercifully whenever he stuttered his thoughts aloud. So, he rarely spoke at all. Fortunately, his young son admired the night sky as much as he did, and they could sit in companionable silence for hours, watching the stars come out one by one, listening to the soft tinkles of bells and the bleating of sheep grazing upon the hillside.

When his brother and son trudged up the hill, his smile died and reformed into a frown. Their expressions and rapid footsteps bespoke the need for haste and—

Daud jogged forward and intercepted them. "What's wrong?"

His son flew into his arms and hugged him around the waist, squeezing him in a fit of joy—or terror—Daud could not say. He grasped the child's arm and stared through the star-filled light into his son's eyes. "What's happened?"

"Oh, Father, the most wonderful thing—angles appeared—from the sky. They gave us news." His son swung an outstretched hand from the star to a cave in a distant hillside and began to tug his father's arm. "Come—see!"

169

"See?" Daud glanced up at Hikmat who had stopped before him, staring at the same cave. "See what?"

With slow reluctance, Hikmat pulled his gaze away and appeared to see his brother for the first time. "Daud, you won't believe me—but the sky was filled with beings, singing and joyous. They announced—the Savior—the Christ is born."

Daud jerked back, his skin prickling. This was not his brother—there was no hint of Hikmat's teasing tone or his haughty expression.

"Come, Father. Let us see the babe!" The child ran ahead like a colt that can't be tethered.

Daud started after him and then glanced back; his voice rose high and strained. "Babe? What babe?"

In the bright night, the undulating movements of many forms froze his voice. A strangled gasp issued from a deep well of terror. Shepherds and folk from leagues around followed the nimble trails leading to that same simple cave, moving as one—at the command of a force Daud could not name.

Like a man rousing from a trance, Hikmat started trotting forward and waved his brother along with a shout. "Come—see!"

—Planet Ingilium—

Bergen stepped away from a compact space shuttle, blinked in the bright glare of the Ingoti sun, and winced at the geometrically perfect city. He rubbed his exposed neck, leaving an irritated red mark. Even when his girlfriend, Yangon, embraced him, his expression refused to soften.

Yangon wrapped her flexible, armored arm around his and tugged him along the broad city walkway. "Long trip?"

Bergen nodded as he tromped along at her side.

Waving to a tall Ingoti beauty crossing the intersection congested with pedestrians, air scooters, and low-level fliers, Yangon sneered and hugged Bergen's arm tighter. "Lee's been asking about you—bragging wretch. Just because she's traveled to distant galaxies. Like that's so special." Yangon glanced at Bergen.

Bergen's fixed gaze had not wavered a millimeter, though he tugged at his chest armor as if a new appliance irritated him.

"You must be worn down. I've got a nutritious meal planned and then—" Rubbing her hand on his arm, she purred. "Well, trust me, the second course will be even better than the first."

~ ~ ~

A stack of metal plates, cups, and cutlery rotated through a wash cycle, as Yangon pulled Bergen to a wide, luxurious couch.

He flopped down with a groan.

She pounced. First, she climbed onto his lap and nibbled his exposed neck. Then she reached—

Bergen stood up and dropped her unceremoniously to the ground. A perplexed frown etched across his forehead. "You ever

171

wonder why we bother? We don't need to eat meals like that. And as for—" He rubbed his neck where she had kissed him and shrugged. "We don't *need* that either."

Yangon's flushed face tightened. "You never complained about my cooking before—or my—"

"I'm not complaining—just wondering. Why are we—trapped?" He clawed at his chest armor.

Yangon stifled a gasp and stumbled to the kitchenette, leaning heavily against the counter. "You've found someone else." With a shudder, she dropped her gaze.

"What? No! I mean, not exactly."

Yangon's head jerked up. She glared at Bergen. "Not exactly? Who—?"

Pulling off his mechanical gloves and unplugging the wrist connectors, Bergen retreated to the couch and perched on the edge. He tapped his emaciated, pale fingers together and peered at the Ingot before him.

Disgust played on Yangon's lips as she stared at his raw hands.

"May I tell you a story?"

Yangon grimaced and slid onto a stool, flexing her mechanical hands over the smooth metal surface. "Whatever."

Bergen stood and paced the white-walled, rectangular room. "Humans are very primitive. I went there to take notes and write an assessment—the usual."

Yangon tapped the datapad embedded in her right arm, scowling.

"But something happened." Halting in mid-step, Bergen's gaze retreated into a memory. "I saw a baby born."

Yangon's lip curled as she rubbed a spot off her breastplate. "Disgusting creatures—giving birth to live young. It's one reason we're so much—"

Bergen blinked. "The baby spoke to me—somehow. His nakedness—his frailty—his sheer honesty—" He staggered.

Her eyes grew into rounded, horrified orbs. "You *exposed* yourself?"

With a wave, Bergen thrust the accusation away. "No. I stayed on the ship. I sent a bot and hid it on one of the animals. But I saw everything. The mother, the father, the birth. The baby's eyes opened, and—for an instant—he looked at me." Bergen swallowed. "He spoke."

"By the Divide, what could an alien infant possibly say?"

"*Live.*" Bergen flopped down on the couch. "I want to *live*—feel hunger, thirst—desire—*love.*" He leaned back and clasped his hand over his eyes.

Yangon rose and glared at the Ingot in front of her. "You've caught some off-world disease, and now you're out of sync." Her lips pursed in disdain. "You'd better see a specialist." Sudden alarm spread over her face. She ran to an alcove and slapped a wall panel. "You better not have given *me* anything—" She rubbed herself all over as an intense light radiated across her body and a disinfectant spray enveloped her.

Bergen shook his head as he climbed to his feet. "I'm not sick. Or out of sync. I've just realized—I'm hardly alive." He started for the door.

Keeping her distance, Yangon stared after him. "Where're you going?"

Passing the window, he pointed to the black, star-filled sky. "I'm going back."

Yangon snorted. "You can't live like a primitive, Ingot. Technology is wired into your very being."

Bergen shrugged. "The Crestas are experimenting on our nursery rejects—maybe they can help me."

Yangon's lip rose in a snarl. "They'll more likely kill you."

"Long as I care—I'll live."

They Might Be Right

Originally published on The Writings of A. K. Frailey
4/20/2018

—OldEarth—

Alessandro gulped as he watched an agonized man pass with a cross hefted on his shoulder. He tugged at his slave collar and waited patiently for the procession to pass. Golgotha was close enough that he could see the crosses already erected and two men hanging in desperate misery. Alessandro closed his eyes and prayed they would die quickly.

Someone jostled his arm, and he glanced up. A woman had run from the crowd and wiped the condemned man's face with her veil. She sobbed as she worked. Alessandro gasped. He has seen this man, this condemned criminal, before.

Jesus.

The memory hit him like a boulder to the chest. He could smell the incense and hear the wailing of the poor widow as she took her son's body to his burial place. Then this same man stepped forward. A few gentle words—and a miracle. The son was alive again. Grief was reborn into perfect joy. Alessandro had relived that moment every day since it had happened.

Now Alessandro watched, stunned, as the crowd followed the procession up the hill. He turned away—he had an errand to run for his master. As he stepped into the narrow, winding street, he looked back and choked. A slave from his youth, taken on a warm, spring day from his home and his family—this was his life.

When Jesus rose on the cross, he stared upon death, his eyes dry.

~ ~ ~

Months later, just when Alessandro finally thought he had put the haunting memory from his mind, he stepped into his master's quarters and froze.

As a Roman citizen of high standing, Felix rarely lost his composure. Today, he stood hunched over his table sobbing like a child. After a moment, the elderly statesman dabbed at his eyes and glanced about.

Alessandro stood in the doorway in perfect obedience. To his confusion, his master smiled and waved him forward.

"Come—don't be afraid."

With firm steps, Alessandro crossed the room, his eyes fixed on his master's face.

Felix sat on the edge of the table, his hands clasped before him. "It is not often that I lose control—but I just received a shock."

Alessandro's collar itched, but he dared not lift a finger.

Felix leaned in and peered into the youth's eyes. "You see, I heard a man preaching in the street today—a Galilean named Peter. He told a marvelous tale—about a man named Jesus of Nazareth rising from the dead. Peter even healed a cripple in Jesus' name." His gaze wandered to the window. "Many have come to believe."

Alessandro's mouth had gone dry as sand.

"I saw Jesus of Nazareth once. Heard all about his miracles. I believed he was—from God."

Alessandro's eyes widened.

"But business pressed, and I did nothing about it. I put him out of my mind." Felix crossed to the window and gazed over the distant hills. "I *did not* crucify him." Tears started in the old Roman's eyes. "I *ignored* him." Clenching his hands together, Felix stepped over to Alessandro, pleading. "God's son, they say—walked among us—and I—did nothing."

Alessandro swallowed. "Even God would not condemn a man for attending to his own business." His hands trembled at his side.

Felix's wan smile chased his grief away. He patted the youth on the arm. "You were a worthy investment—I knew that when I first saw you as a boy." Felix returned to the window. "No, I do not feel condemned. I feel—lost."

Shaking his head and squaring his shoulders, Felix returned to business. "I have a message you must take." He pinched a small parchment off his table and handed it to his slave.

After bowing, Alesandro turned to leave.

Felix called out. "One more question—I know you can't answer—but I feel it must be asked."

Alessandro paused, suddenly afraid.

"Will God—ever come again?"

Walking along the narrow street, Alessandro knew—that question would ring in his ears to the end of his days.

~ ~ ~

A sunbeam slanted across a quiet hillside where a gentle slope led to a grassy expanse, a world of hyssop, daffodils, lupine, iris, and buzzing insects, two figures appeared. One grandfather figure with gray hair and a slight stoop nodded, beaming at a young man with golden brown hair, brilliant blue eyes, and the physique of a young Adonis. They were both dressed in the simple garments of common shepherds.

"Very good, Cerulean! You maintained your shape perfectly! It's not every Luxonian who can travel as an alien species and keep their proper form. You look every inch the human boy—a little *too perfect,* maybe—but we can adjust that. Remember, humans become either enamored or jealous at the sight of physical perfection."

The youth nodded even while his gaze traveled the parameter of their setting. "We're safe here?"

"Of course. I've had eons of experience at this sort of thing. Nothing to be afraid of."

Cerulean clasped his hands together and waited.

A few scattered sheep crested one of the far hills. Cerulean's eyes widened.

The old man hefted a shepherd's staff and nudged the boy along. "Now remember, just act natural—like you have your own business to attend to, and no one will bother you."

A shepherd appeared at the top of a distant hill. He peered at them and waved.

Cerulean glanced at his father. "Teal? I believe that man is trying to get our attention."

"Just keep walking—he'll ignore us if we go away."

Cerulean padded across the grassy pastureland, his gaze wandering back to the man on the hill.

Teal prodded the boy on the shoulders. "Don't look. Never engage in eye contact unless you want to meet someone—which you never will. You're just here to observe, take careful note of everything significant, and inform the Supreme Council of your findings when you return to Lux."

Cerulean snuck another glance, but, as his father had predicted, the man had returned to the care of his sheep. He sighed. "We could have gone anywhere on the planet; why—?"

Teal yelped and gripped his son's shoulder. "Stop a moment. I've got something caught between my toes. Panting, he cleared his foot of a trailing weed and then pointed to the blue sky. "Do you remember the story I told you and your mother about the miracle healer, heralded by the magnificent star at his birth? It was noted by every intelligent species this side of the Divide."

Rubbing his forehead, Cerulean frowned. "As I remember, the man was murdered—by his own people."

"True, but that wasn't the end of the story. The people in these lands believed that he rose again and lived on in a new form." Teal's gaze scanned the cloudless sky. "I've been waiting for him to return."

"You think he will?"

Teal sighed. "Three generations have passed. I have little hope left. But they say that he lives in the hearts of believers. I have even heard that he comes as food for—"

"Food?" Cerulean's eyebrows rose.

"Not in human form—but as bread." Teal shrugged. "It's hard to explain."

"Despite your official reports, humans sound rather barbaric."

Teal chuckled. "Beware, humans grow on you. They're surprising—they have unexpected strength, and they believe in miracles."

Cerulean glanced at the crest of the hill where the shepherd reappeared with a young boy at his side. "I wonder what they believe."

"You will be a guardian soon enough, and experience is the greatest teacher. Just remember—" He nudged his son forward.

Cerulean plodded along, his gaze focused on the crest of another hill. "What?"

"They might be right."

Impossible Beings

Originally published on The Writings of A. K. Frailey
5/31/2018

—OldEarth—

Rome 450 AD

As Lidia plopped her hands into a heavy clay bowl of flour, a dusty spray plumed into the air, casting a million specks into the sunlight slanting across the room from a high rectangular window.

Her daughter, Marcia, stared up enchanted. Her lips parted in a soft smile, while her eyes danced in rhythm to the twirling, sparking mini-universe spreading wide throughout the kitchen. Her voice dropped to a reverent whisper. "Papa says the world goes on forever—is that true?"

After thoroughly dusting a ball of dough, Lidia pressed it flat on the kneading trough. She grunted, her eyes on her work, but her gaze turned inward. "Your father says a great many things—some he oughtn't." She flipped the dough over and shrugged. Her focus cleared, and she spared a glance at the little girl. "You know how he is."

Laying an open palm on the table, Marcia waited in hopeful expectation.

With a snort, Lidia ripped off a hunk and dropped it into the child's hands. "Don't knead it too much, remember. The soldiers return today— by the gods' mercy—and he'll enjoy a nice soft bread for a change."

Marcia eased her fingers onto the pliant dough and allowed her hands to undulate like deep-sea fronds waving in a gentle current. A studious frown etched across her brow. "Will he stay long this time?"

Placing the shaped dough onto a baking tray, Lidia wiped the excess flour from the edges. "These are ruinous times for soldiers and high born alike. Rome has lost her footing, and the gods are not pleased. Invaders break in the front door while useless slaves run out the back."

"But Papa says that Rome is invincible. We dare the impossible."

Lidia shoved a smaller tray in front of her daughter and watched her lay the dough straight. A flicker of a smile swept across her face and just as quickly vanished. She retreated to a large oven set in the back wall and slid the two trays on a shelf. Clapping the dust from her hands, she jutted her chin in the direction of a pail of water. "Wash up and go outside now. Keep an eye out for Papa."

Marcia dunked her hands in the cold water and scrubbed away the shreds of sticky dough. After rinsing twice, she patted her hands dry and held them up for her mother's inspection. "We *are* invincible—aren't we?"

Bending with her hands on her thighs, Lidia fixed her daughter in the eye. "Truth is, no one born of woman is invincible. Only the gods be invincible—and even they suffer loss and death." She straightened and washed her hands, splashing drops on the dusty floor. "We dare the impossible—true—while we may." She nodded to the threshold leading to a garden path. "But don't worry your father with such notions. He's suffered on every side, and I won't have him lose his faith as well."

Marcia's gaze wandered back to the sunlit kitchen. The sparking universe had disappeared into shadows. She blinked and set her jaw. The entire Roman world might crumble—but a miniature universe floated in hidden mystery all around her—if only she dared the impossible.

—Planet Helm—

Bhuaci Capitol

Bhuaci are a gelatinous race that can mold themselves into the likeness of a variety of races, both sentient and not. Bhuaci are often called the perfect race as they often mold themselves to the physical ideal of any race they encounter.

Sitting at a large ornate desk with a highly decorated border, Crimson dipped her quill in ink, wrote a long scrawling line, and grinned at the result.

A cherubic boy with a dimple in each cheek, golden curls, and twirling a blooming forsythia branch stopped before the red-hued, lanky Bhuaci beauty and grinned. "What 'cha doing?"

Crimson peered from her parchment to the childish form in front of her and snarled, "Get away from me you—absurdity."

The cherub's eyes gleamed in anything-but-innocent delight. He swept his dainty fingers down his fulsome figure. "Don't you like it? You're

183

always telling me to get a new look. Well, cherubs happen to be all the rage these days."

Crimson let her pen fall from her fingers as her eyes widened in disgust. Her snarl morphed into a snort. "You always traipse after the newest fashion—never really live in any form—just change to keep up with the crowd." Retrieving her pen, she punctuated the air. "You'd take an insect shape on a dare—and get stepped on before the day was out."

The cherub's eyes glimmered and narrowed as his body grew, adding weight, muscle, color, and masculinity. Now towering above the Bhuaci female as a gleaming warrior wearing a sleeveless tunic—every fiber of his perfect form, from his deep-set blue, determined chin, squared shoulders, barrel chest, and muscular legs screamed classic male beauty.

Crimson tilted her head and considered the specimen before her. She sniffed. "You might have hit on something this time, Kane." Her mouth twitched. "Let's see how long it lasts."

Kane sauntered to the high desk and leaned over Crimson's shoulder. "You never answered my question."

With a plaintive sigh, Crimson picked up her pen and dipped it in the inkpot. "I'm trying to work—if you don't mind."

"With a feather?"

"It's a quill, idiot." Crimson pointed to a sign over the door. "Record's office—remember? I transcribe ships' logs. Today I have to transcribe Longjur's hasty notes and send them—"

A blush crept over Kane's face. "Longjur? He's been observing Earth—right?"

"Yep, and by the Divide, he has a lot to say! Mostly it's as boring as watching a cactus grow in the dry season. But this part—"

Kane's gaze scanned the nearly empty page. "Where?"

Crimson frowned. "Well, I was just getting to it when you interrupted. I have it here." She tapped a panel embedded in the desk. "But I'm making a formal copy for the Kestrel Committee. I thought ink on parchment would do nicely to reflect the culture and add a bit of authenticity and charm. They'll look it over before making recommendations—"

Kane shook his head. "Forget all that! What did he say? Is he going back?"

Crimson slapped her cheek and rolled her eyes. "He went on and on about silly details—emperors and warriors and their never-ending battles, women and men sweating in the hot sun and toiling for their food, and the most ignorant ceremonies I've ever heard of! But there was one point of interest..." She checked her notes, running her finger along the lines. "About a little girl, sunlight, and a hidden—"

Kane groaned, his shoulders sagging. "I want to go there—someday." He shrugged. "It's why I take on so many forms—for practice. I'd love to explore that system. Humanoids seem so—impossible." He peered down at Crimson and their eyes met. "You know what I mean?"

Crimson tapped the panel, a lopsided smile wavering on her lips. "Don't despair. You must have read Longjur's mind. He said that exact thing—and I quote: 'They are impossible beings, yet they bring their faith to fruition.'"

Kane leaned in and stared deep into Crimson's eyes. "So, you think I might go—"

Crimson chuckled and returned to her work. "You'd fit right in."

We Could Cry

Originally published on The Writings of A. K. Frailey
6/15/2018

(An early version of an *OldEarth Melchior Encounter* chapter)

Frozen to the core, Melchior sat slouch-shouldered at the table; tendrils of steam from his venison stew rose before him. He took a tentative sip and burned his tongue.

Gideon hurried into the hall, his arms swinging at his side, a smile radiating from his face. "Father! Good news!"

Melchior pursed his lips.

Settling next to his father on the bench, Gideon peered from the old man to the stew and grinned. Lifting the bowl, he blew away the steam. After a few hearty puffs, he placed the bowl before his father with a flourish. "You're right. God takes care of everything!"

"Not always."

Gideon shook his head. "Well, this time. Wilfred told the Prince about the church, and guess what? You can't imagine."

"Probably not."

"The prince offered to support the building. He even gave me gold to show his sincerity." Gideon drew out a bag and poured heavy coins onto the table. "Prince Omar believes that the church must be free to serve God without a king's influence. He's going to persuade his father to visit, too."

Melchior swallowed as he envisioned an entourage of foreign kings arriving at his humble abode. "Father Caedmon named you rightly.

You're a warrior meant to spread the word of God, but with a pen, not a sword." Melchior's frown returned. "What about studying in Rome?"

Gideon's eyes glowed. "Perhaps I don't need to go. With good scholars, we can teach here. Men might come from all over the world to see what we have preserved, what we have remembered...for the glory of God."

Melchior sighed as images of ruins, mud-caked roads, and ignorant men rose in his mind.

Gideon grasped his father's cold, feeble hand. "You see. It's a miracle! And through the help of a foreign king!"

Melchior's blank stare through red-rimmed eyes proclaimed what he did not see.

"Your father named you *Melchior* after a foreign king who served God through a gift of gold. This time it will be a king's son, but a king's power nonetheless, who serves God through a gift of gold." Gideon clapped his hands together. "What a wonderful sense of humor God has!"

Melchior sat motionlessly. His stew was quite cool by now. He swallowed and remembered his father's gentle face as he peered up at him, sitting on the old man's knee as a boy.

"Never give up, Melchior, for God is never outdone in generosity. His strength reaches to men—through men. God never abandons His own."

Pushing his stew to the side, Melchior stared at his happy son. The tears that slipped down his cheeks warmed his face.

~~~

A silent, invisible being sat at the far end of the table, entranced. Omega itched to take on human form, but he knew the rules. Mother had explained observation techniques very carefully, and Abbas had outlined the horrors of alien exposure in vivid detail. If he wanted a world of his own someday, he must study hard and not take risks.

Appearing as nothing more than a flicker of wind, Omega rose from the table, circled around the old man, and bent low to examine the tears. *Awesome things—tears.* Fearing spontaneous combustion from sheer exuberance, Omega returned to his own world.

—Mystery Planet—

Bright flames flickered over huge logs set into a fireplace large enough to roast a full-grown ox. Lush tapestries and rich oil paintings adorned the lofty walls while heavy wooden trestle tables lined the perimeter.

Appearing as an elderly human in a long robe, wearing a red skullcap, Abbas reclined on an ornate couch with enough pillows to satisfy a Greek god. Studying a painting—the Mona Lisa—propped on a stand at his side, he tapped his fingers against his lips, a minor scowl etched across his brow.

Omega strode into the great hall, bent and kissed his father on the forehead, and tilted his head at the Mona Lisa. "Figure her out yet?"

Abbas rose and waved a languid hand. "She's not half as interesting as the men who find her fascinating." Abbas pointed to the painting. "Do you know that Leonardo—the artist—painted her to represent the ideal of happiness?"

A grin played on Omega's lips. "He's quite wrong. I believe I've discovered ideal happiness—in tears."

In a fluid motion, Abbas rose and strode to a side table filled with golden goblets and a carafe of pink liquid. "Been to Earth again—have we?" He poured healthy dashes into goblets and handed one to his son. "You realize that we have to find our own medium of happiness—each and every day. It's not something one discovers once and for all." He took a smooth sip, eyeing his son over the rim.

In one gulp, Omega downed his drink and tossed the goblet into the fire.

His father frowned.

Flopping onto the couch, Omega crossed his legs and leaned back. He closed his eyes. "I watched a young man turn his father from agony to ecstasy with mere words. He spoke of God as if he knew Him personally, and he drew hope from despair. The old man's tears redeemed him." Jumping to his feet, Omega crossed the room and poured himself another drink. "I find that fascinating—even though I hardly understood a word he said." He gulped down the second drink as quickly as the first, but before he could throw the goblet, his father snatched it from his hand.

"You're a child, Omega, fascinated by new experiences." He placed the goblet back on the table. "Even though we have power—we must not waste it. You are too hasty. You—"

"But that's why they fascinate me! They are creatures of passion and intellect, yet as far below us as their amphibians are below them. But still, they make such music, such poetry—" He swung around and pointed at the Mona Lisa. "Such glorious art! It resonates within me."

Abbas lifted the painting off the stand and placed it securely between two masterpieces on the wall. His frown deepened.

"Ay, father! Do you think that perhaps they're right? Maybe they were created by the same God—and that's why—"

"Don't forget yourself! You were sent to study—not to emulate—aliens. We worship no gods—or beings—beyond ourselves. That's how *we* became so powerful. We're the best the universe has to offer."

Turning to the fire and running his fingers through the flames, Omega chuckled. "Yes, Father. That's why we copy their paintings, eat their food, sit at their tables, live in their castles, and wear their skins. We study them—" His smile faded. "And wish we could cry."

Of Gods and Men

Originally published on The Writings of A. K. Frailey
6/29/2018

—OldEarth—

China 1041 AD

Bi Shang scooped a handful of sticky clay and set it on a wooden sideboard. Using sharpened sticks, he pulled off sections, and with sure and steady hands, shaped each piece into thin-edged characters. Bending low, his eyebrows furrowed over the intense work, but a lilting hum escaped his lips.

A thin, young man draped in flowing pantaloons and a loose, gray tunic shuffled into the bright room, keeping close to the wall. His large eyes followed the older man with wide-eyed curiosity. "What're you doing?"

Undisturbed, Bi Shang arranged each character on an iron baking tray. When the tray was full, he straightened and rubbed his back with one hand. With the other, he beckoned. "Come, Jian."

Jian stepped forward, tilting his head to see better.

"I'm preserving human intelligence."

Jian's eyes narrowed. "*My* intelligence?"

With a chuckle, Bi Shang snatched a piece of wood from a basket and laid it carefully on a pile of glowing embers in a bake oven embedded in the wall. "Hmm. Yours and your children's as well."

Snorting, Jian waved the thought away. "You're teasing."

As the flickering flames grew, Bi Shang lifted a rack from the floor and placed it inside the oven. He grabbed a bowl of water and sprinkled the flames, taming them into smoky heat.

The boy's eyes widened again. "But why—?"

"Because, this is delicate work, and I don't want my characters to go up in flames." Satisfied, Bi Shang carefully laid the tray on the rack over the radiant heat. With a contented sigh, he bent low and pointed. "See those shapes?"

Jian nodded.

"They represent the thoughts of men across the world." His eyes twinkled. "And when we put many thoughts together—we shape both men and world."

An angry pout formed on Jian's lips. "You only tell me such stories because I'm small for my age."

With a gentle hand, Bi Shang squeezed the boy's shoulder. "On the contrary. I'm sharing great power with you. When my characters bake hard and strong, I'll set them out for the world to read and ponder. Thoughts grow upon thoughts, and our people will know what wise men of the world believed."

Stretching forth a tentative finger, Jian touched the clay and rubbed it between his fingers.

Tapping the boy's arm, Bi Shang grinned. "Someday, if you watch and learn, you'll know the thoughts of many and share your thoughts with the universe—wisdom to last beyond human sight."

"Forever?" Jian squinted as if trying to see the edge of unlimited eons. "My thoughts are like the wind." His gaze fell to the dusty floor. "And can sometimes be evil."

Bi Shang stroked his face. "You are more honest than most." Returning to his work, he turned his back to the boy. "Evil thoughts can teach us, too." He glanced over his shoulder. "For none are barred from their embrace." He sighed. "Though the wind sometimes uproots the old, it also carries in invigorating air."

Jian shook his head, a worried frown etched across his forehead. "Such a power is for the gods and their anointed."

Bi Shang nodded as he lifted his sharp sticks and began to shape a new character. He bent over his work in silent intensity.

Jian shuffled toward the door.

After placing new characters on a fresh tray, Bi Shang lifted his finger. "Before you leave, look at these." He beckoned Jian forward.

Returning, Jian bent over the iron tray. A new light entered his eyes. "What do they mean?"

"Free—Spirit." Bi Shang fixed his gaze on the boy. "We choose what we believe."

Jian nodded; his bright eyes fastened on the figures. "Of gods and men."

~~~

Sterling, a Luxonian disguised in the rough garb of a Chinese peasant, slapped a mosquito on his arm and frowned at the sight of blood. "Damn insects. Stupid humans! I'm so bored I could—"

"Sir?" Teal, a younger Luxonian dressed in a matching style, stepped out from behind a bush.

He nodded toward a tree. "If you need to use—uh—want a little privacy—"

"I'd rather disintegrate."

Smothering a smile as he rubbed a hand across his face, Teal nodded respectfully. "I doubt that'll be necessary." He started toward a sloping hill crowned with a copse of woods. "Though you did have five cups of tea."

Laboring alongside his companion, Sterling blew air between his lips. "I keep thinking these new world voyages will stimulate me—invigorate my lagging spirit. But instead, everything is so blasted uncomfortable—it's either hot and humid or dry and cold." He tugged at his collar. "These ridiculous clothes scratch unmercifully, and the insect life—"

Teal huffed as he neared the crest. "But you enjoyed the tea and cakes—don't deny it. And, you must admit, watching humans' first foray into printing was rather fascinating." With eager steps, he entered the woods.

Sterling tripped and grabbed a branch for balance. "I hate hiding in dark corners. And I'd hardly call a grown man attempting to convince a pathetic child that his clay characters imply a universal achievement—fascinating." He snapped the twig off the tree and pounded further into the dense woods. "Really, I wonder if becoming a judge is worth all the risk."

Yelping, Teal stopped and leaned against a tree. He dug a stone out of his sandal. "You have to understand the various life forms in your jurisdiction. How else will you make fair assessments?"

Sterling shuffled from one foot to another, his frown deepening. "I understand that. I just don't like all the needless hardship. Why couldn't I have been offered a position on Helm? Shapeshifters have much better sensibilities." He swallowed and his face flushed. "I can't stand it."

Teal glanced around. "We're safe here. Go ahead—return to Luxonian form."

"No time!" Sterling rushed behind a tree.

Teal snatched a nut from a tree and studied it thoughtfully, ignoring Sterling's long, shuddering sigh.

Wandering like a man lost in a dream, Sterling circled toward Teal. "I never imagined such relief—"

Teal pushed away from the trunk. "If you're ready, we should make our report. Do a good job, and you'll make a Supreme Judge someday." He grinned. "As guardian, I'll always be here to help."

Sterling threw up his hands in renewed anguish. "But I haven't got anything to report! It's all so inconsequential."

A brooding frown spread across Teal's face. "Open your mind." Teal strode closer and looked Sterling in the eyes. "Think about what you've seen—all of humanity's challenges. They suffer from their corporeal bodies and their primitive living conditions—yet they manage to invent new ways to express themselves and preserve knowledge. They work hard, practice discipline and patience, endure pain, and, yes, enjoy relief. And, from the look on the young man's face, they also know ecstatic joy." He waved his hands as if to encompass the entire planet. "I'd say that was consequential."

Sterling peered up at the bright sky filtered between the leafy branches. "Perhaps you're right." He grinned as he leveled his gaze at Teal. "Supreme Judge, eh?" He glanced around, his smile fading. "Only if I survive."

That's What Turns Heads

Originally published on The Writings of A. K. Frailey
7/13/2018

—OldEarth—

1492 Hispaniola

"Lord love you, young'un. You've got a lot to learn."

The sailor's brawny muscles gleamed in the bright sunshine as he hoisted a coiled rope over his shoulder and headed to the group arranging gear on shore.

The boy squinted, staring at the glinting, sandy shore and the violent green vegetation before him. After months on ship, the dazzling spectacle stole his breath. "But we're safe here, Diego? I mean—"

Diego called to the sweating men ahead. "Pedro wants to know if he's safe now."

Glancing back, the gathered sailors laughed, smiles creasing their weather-worn faces. One man waved. "We're never safe—until we settle in our grave, Niño. You outta know that."

A dark-haired native holding an armload of goods stepped from the foliage. The sailors backed up, glancing aside at each other.

Pedro raced forward and joined the sailors. "What does he want?"

"Trade most likely."

Diego peered back.

No one else moved.

After swiping a sword from a neat stack, Diego stepped forward and intercepted the native. He held out the sword in an offering.

A bronze-skinned child scuttled forward and laid a cloth on the ground. Grinning, the native laid a bundle of skeins, a woven cage of brightly colored parrots, and a bundle of darts tied together before the sailors. Four more native men stepped forward and stood on each side of the offering.

The elder of the group reached for the sword, unwittingly gripping the blade. He winced as it cut deep and blood seeped down his hand.

Pedro gasped.

Diego muttered. "Not an auspicious beginning."

Another sailor shrugged. "Not for them, anyway."

—Planet Crestar—

Ark, wearing a long, white apron over his green bio-suit, rubbed his eyes and stepped away from the three-meter magnifier. An open dissection tube extended from the west wall. "By the Divide, I'll never get through this data-stream."

A ding sounded, and Ark's head swiveled, his gaze landing on the door. "Come in."

A Crestonian with bright red cilia, obviously artificially colored, and a deep purple bio-suit ambled in and offered a lopsided grin. "Nearly done?" He lifted one tentacle and dropped a bundle of data-strips onto a standing tray. "You know what they say—no rest for the weary."

Ark's tentacles curled, his bulbous brown eyes narrowing. "Not with you around." He bowed in mock respect. "Thank you, Ungle. Share my joy with those who—"

Ungle waved a tentacle. "Oh, don't sound so bitter." He stumped over to a wall cupboard and slid the door aside. After lifting a green canister, he popped the top and sniffed. "Is this fresh?"

"It was yesterday."

With a shrug, Ungle poured a significant dollop into his breather helm and hummed. "Not bad." Replacing the canister, he turned to Ark and peered at the magnifier. "You can't blame them. After all, your suggestion turned stomachs as well as heads."

Ark slapped a wall console and the magnifier dimmed. "I didn't suggest anything. I just noted that human interaction with foreigners would do them greater good in the long run than isolation. They'll kill each other for a time, but after that, they'll interbreed and—"

"Tut-tut! That's where you started turning stomachs."

"I wasn't saying we should interbreed with aliens—that was Irbid's weird editorial. You know how he likes to liven up the news. He'll theorize any ol' thing to get a reaction."

"You have to admit, he's usually right. At least in the core point."

"And I'm right too. Interaction with aliens has been good for us. Think of everything I learned from the Luxonians."

Ungle lifted a tentacle. "Please. You're missing the point you related in the last debriefing cycle." The ridges above his eyes rose precariously.

"Remember? The native took the sword and cut his hand?"

"He didn't know any better. He'll learn."

After pointing to the data-strips, Uncle waved as he headed for the door. "To grab the sword from the hilt—and swing it properly. Yes, I know. That's what turns heads—and drops them to the ground."

The Play Is the Thing

Originally published on The Writings of A. K. Frailey
7/27/2018

—OldEarth—

1666 London, England

"It was an excellent play—best I ever saw." Being taller than average, Samuel peered over the evening throng on a dim, misty street corner and waved to a coachman. "Never before did I did see the King's House so full."

His companion, Mr. Creed, smiled as he stood close, his hands clasped before him. "Becky Marshall has outdone herself. The Cardinall will meet grand success, certainly."

Samuel glanced aside, his good mood expanding his heart. "Come and have supper with me. There's bound to be some meat pasties left, and you can spend the night."

With a cringe of regret, Creed ducked his head. "Not this time. I've got a meeting in the morning." Watching the coach draw near, he stepped back. "But I'll ride till your house."

Oblivious to the danger, Samuel stood on the curb and as the coach jolted to a halt, mud splashed on Samuel's best grey suit. His eyes widened in fury. "Oh, bloody hell. I'm presenting before the committee tomorrow."

Creed only shrugged in helpless innocence and the two men climbed aboard. A memory from a comedic part of the play lightened Samuel's mood. With a mild chuckle, he wiped the worst of the mud from his pant legs. "Jane can see to it in the morning." He stretched out and sighed. "I shouldn't have wasted another whole evening, but—"

Creed patted an enormous yawn. "We work hard and get little recompense for our efforts, so a little fun won't do us any harm." He waved a teasing finger. "As that Shakespeare fellow said, 'The play's the thing.'"

His eyebrows rising, Samuel shrugged. "Oh, *him*. I like his work well enough, but so much depends on the presentation." The coach bolted over a series of bumps jerking Samuel further down his seat. "You can have the best lines in the world, but if they're read by a fool, foolish they will be."

Creed nodded. "Or the opposite. Take the king. When he speaks nonsense, everyone oohs and ahs as if pearls of wisdom drop from his lips."

The coach jerked to a stop as another coach crossed its path.

Samuel closed his eyes, folding his hands behind his head. "The simple truth is—Plays make life worth living."

Mr. Creed chuckled. "To escape reality?"

His eyes flicked open; Samuel stared at Creed. "To make sense of reality. In a play, we dare to tell a truth that'd normally get a man killed."

Stifling another yawn, Creed rested his head on his hand. "Playwrights must pray that kings are blind as well as foolish."

"A safe bet, if you ask me." Samuel scratched his chin, eyeing Creed carefully. "There's another play tomorrow. Want to go?"

Mr. Creed slapped his cheeks through another enormous yawn. "What's playing?'

"Does it matter?"

The coach creaked to a halt in front of a stately house, and Mr. Creed stepped out, followed by Samuel, who tossed a coin to the driver.

Samuel carefully stepped around the puddles and strode up the cobblestone walk.

Mr. Creed called after him. "Till tomorrow then."

Samuel chuckled as he opened his door, never looking back. "The play's the thing."

~ ~ ~

Teal gripped his son's shoulder and led him across the muddy street. Dressed as common English laborers, they watched Mr. Creed amble down the road, his steps fading into the London night.

Cerulean peered into his father's face. "I didn't understand the play they watched. The audience laughed at things that weren't even funny."

Teal patted Cerulean's shoulder and nudged him down the road beyond Samuel's neat, white house. "Humor does not translate well from one culture to another." He shrugged. "But from the description, that play was meant as a tragedy."

"Why in the universe would anyone want to reenact a tragedy?"

"Humans have peculiar tastes." Teal tugged Cerulean into a shadow as another coach rattled by. "Personally, I think it's how they process their existence." He glanced down at the young

Luxonian. "Did you hear what they were saying in the coach?"

"I never hear well as an insect." Cerulean grinned. "But I changed into a mouse as soon as I was under the seat, and then I could hear very well indeed."

"You're learning." Teal patted Cerulean's back.

A woman's scream tore through the London streets.

Cerulean jumped forward.

Teal gripped his arm. "Don't get involved."

The woman screamed again. Men's voices jeered in drunken laughter.

Cerulean tugged, trying to pull free. "But someone's getting hurt."

Teal shook his head and lifted his hand, his index finger pointing to the moonlit sky. "We're guardians of our world—not theirs." He pulled Cerulean closer and peered into his eyes. "Trust me; there's nothing we can do. We'd only make matters worse if we got involved."

Cerulean jerked free, heaving deep breaths, his eyes wide and alarmed.

Distant murmurs turned to chuckles and fell into silence.

Teal beckoned to his son. "It's time we went home."

Cerulean's shoulders drooped in defeat. "But what was the point of coming tonight? We didn't learn anything."

"On the contrary. I have a brilliant idea for a new presentation to give the Supreme Council." Teal chuckled.

Leaping over a puddle, Cerulean drew closer. "What'll it be called?"

Teal took Cerulean's hand. "Guess."

Staring up at his father, the starlight twinkling in his eyes, Cerulean grinned. "The play's the thing."

A Fresh Thought

Originally published on The Writings of A. K. Frailey
8/10/2018

—OldEarth—

"For all the difficulty of philosophy seems to consist in this—from the phenomena of motions to investigate the forces of Nature, and then from these forces to demonstrate the other phenomena..." ~Isaac Newton

Robert sat hunched over a wooden table shoved against the wall of a dimly lit pub. He stared at a cream-colored pamphlet and tugged his fingers through his hair, pulling a couple strands from his head.

Flames from a stone hearth sent a flickering glow across the smoky, half-filled room as voices murmured in a multitude of evening conversations.

A woman in a stained, serviceable dress strolled over and perched her hand on her hip, a damp rag gripped tight in her fist. "You'll go blind, staring like that." She tapped the page with one dismissive finger. "Not worth it, I say." She hitched a thumb behind her. "Look at Henry. He's got the right idea. Barkeepers make money hand over fist and sleep in comfortable beds."

Henry, a thin, wiry man, polished a heavy mug and set it on the counter beside a stack of empty plates.

Robert lifted his blanched face and stared through red-rimmed eyes. "You don't

207

understand, Isabel. This is the greatest revelation to humanity since...I don't know. Maybe since God created the world."

A chuckle from across the room turned heads. A tall, hefty man rose from a barstool and sauntered closer. "There's them that can meddle in such things and those who'd best keep their eyes on their work."

Isabel nodded. "You tell 'em, William. He won't listen to me."

William laid a meaty hand on Robert's shoulder. "Your pa's looking for you, surely."

Robert glanced from Isabel to William, the line of his mouth hardening. "Pa sent me to school to learn—he don't want me to stop, just because times are tough."

Grunting, William hitched his thumbs in his belt and straightened, throwing his head back like a man about to tell a tall tale. "Times are more than tough. Plague, fire, wars, and famine are constant companions. A man's life is bitter and short." He bent down and stared earnestly into Robert's eyes. "Your pa is a dreamer but getting older by the day." William whistled through a gap in a missing tooth. "I did my time aboard a ship, nearly died more often than I cared to count. But grace, hard work, and sticking to my business saved me." He glanced aside, a wince of pain shooting across his face. "And those I cared about."

Robert scowled. "And how were you treated for your service, William? Never honestly paid, were you? Was it right that so many good men died needlessly?"

Like a clap of thunder, William smacked the table, turning every head in the pub, his gaze hard and his eyes glowing. He spat his words. "That little book going to make the world more just? Going to give a man his rightful due?"

Her grip tightened, water dripped from Isabel's rag, her gaze darted from William to Robert.

Robert shoved back his chair and rose. "If you mean, will knowledge pay a decent wage, no, probably not. But will it allow a man to feel like a man—to think like a man?" Robert closed the pamphlet and tucked it in his coat pocket. "Then, yes. Knowledge will give a man his due."

William scratched his neck and shook his head, wrinkles crinkling at the corners of his eyes. "Never thought to say that the son of Giles Churchwarden was a fool, but if you spend all your days trying to understand the likes of that book, you've earned the title, make no mistake."

From the back of the room, Henry lifted a mug and laughed. "We'll come to the same end, Willie boy. Don't begrudge the man his grand ideas. Twas a foolish God who thought of us, remember." He beckoned Robert to the bar. "If you ever understand even a bit of it, share the likes with those of us who enjoy a fresh thought."

Robert met the barkeeper's gaze. "I'll tend my pa's farm during the day, but we'll exchange a thought or two in the evening, Henry." Darting a glance from William to Isabel, Robert crossed the threshold and stepped into the starry night. He sighed. "Life's less bitter that way."

A gigantic hall lit with hundreds of candles shone in reflected glory. Each piece of polished furniture gleamed, and colorful tapestries hung from high ceilings, covering the stone walls. Two large trestle tables dominated the central space, while a dais occupied the far end. Huge logs from full-grown trees blazed in the fireplaces at opposite ends of the room.

Shopkeepers, smiths, farmers, cow herders, carpenters, cobblers, fishermen, husbands and fathers, wives and mothers, serving women and serving men, bustled about, some eating, some chatting, some working, some resting from a long day's work.

Dressed like a fine lord in a short white tunic and a flowing burgundy robe, a young, handsome-looking man sauntered beside his father and gazed around the room. "You must admit, it was a pleasant experience. There's nothing like seeing them in their native environment to help us understand how to best care for them."

His gray-haired father climbed the three steps to the jewel-encrusted throne and plunked down in apparent exhaustion. "I think you missed the man's point, Omega."

Omega chuckled and threw himself down on the smaller throne to the right of his father. "Which man?" He lifted his hand. "You mean Robert?" He tapped his fingers together steeple-style. "It's true, I should give these beings more to think about. But—" He grinned. "They seem so content."

"You save them from certain death, and they're grateful. They play your game and live like this because they need you." The old man stared at his son. "But remember what the barkeep said."

Omega frowned. "He wanted a fresh thought now and again. That shouldn't be too hard." He laid his hand over his father's. "You're always coming up with fresh ideas, Abbas."

The old man pursed his lips. "Robert remembered who created them." Abbas beckoned to the serving man. "A stout ale for me and milk for my son."

Omega scowled and opened his mouth, but Abbas interrupted.

"They may think that God is a fool for creating them free." Abbas rubbed his temple. "But by far, more's the fool who tries to keep them captive."

Omega lifted his arms as if embracing the entire hall full of people. "They would've died on Earth. This may be a mirage—but it's a good mirage. At least they're alive."

"Lies—even good lies—never satisfy for long. Remember Newton? There was a man who could not be satisfied with mere appearance."

The serving man placed a golden tankard into Omega's waiting hand.

Abbas drank deeply and wiped his foamy lips with the back of his hand. "Best be careful, son. The turning of the human mind is no less startling than the turning of a planet. And a whole lot less predictable."

Speck in the Universe

Originally published on The Writings of A. K. Frailey
8/24/2018

—OldEarth—

Pete, flushed and sweaty from running across the playground, huffed as he caught up with his friend. "Mom said that they're spreading space junk all over the atmosphere, and aliens'll get really mad. Maybe annihilate us all cause of it."

Bert crossed his arms and shifted onto one leg, bracing himself on the chain-link fence. "Aw, that's stupid. Those NASA folks are experts. They know what they're doing. Sides, we're alone in the universe." He pointed at the blue sky. "Not even plants up there. Just lots of rocks flying about in ginormous empty space."

His hand perched on his hips; Pete's cheeks darkened. "That's what you say. But I'm positive that aliens exist. I read a whole book on alien abductions. Really cool."

Bert lowered his gaze and narrowed his eyes. "You'd be okay with getting dissected and studied and then put back together and sent home to have weird dreams for the rest of your life?"

Pete shrugged. "I'd go to an analyst. Mom's analyst tells her what her dreams mean and where she's really from—"

"Please. I'd die if I had to tell anyone my dreams."

Bert scrunched his eyebrows together and kicked a stone. "Still, I'd rather take a chance on being dissected than believe we're alone."

Sticking the edge of his tennis shoe into the fifth row of links, Pete hefted himself up and climbed to the top. He swung a leg over and perched on the bar. "What's so bad about being alone? Even if there were aliens, we'd just be a speck to them." He peered down. "You saw what Mr. James showed us...solar systems, galaxies, universes...it went on and on. We're lost in it all—invisible."

Bert propped his hand over his eyes, blocking the sun. "You'd better get down. They upped the suspension time."

Pete laughed. "Suspension? Who cares? I'd just listen to music and watch stuff. Better than listening to teachers yammer on about things I'll have to fact-check later. Like it matters."

Bert leaned on the fence, his face tired and drawn. He wiped his sweaty brow. "I guess that's why I like aliens. Maybe they'd care. Maybe they'd think we do matter—even though we're just a tiny speck in the universe."

A man called from across the yard. "Hey! Off that fence, boy, or I'll have you running laps after school."

Pete scrambled down and frowned, his gaze darting from the cement to the angry teacher. "Sheesh. You'd think he owned it!"

Bert squinted at the man, who turned and strode away. "Kinda does. He's in charge of the yard—he'll get blamed if we damage school property."

A shrill bell rang, sending a flurry of students to the door.

Pete slumped across the yard. "Who cares?"

Bert followed along beside his friend, watching the teachers line up, waiting for their students. "I think they do."

—Planet Ingilium—

Zuri, dressed in a battered mechanical exoskeleton, hefted a large cylindrical object over his shoulder and nodded to the Cresta before him. "Thanks, Uv. I heard they don't make these parts anymore."

Uv bowed with his four tentacles wrapped daintily behind his thick middle. His stained bio-suit bulged at the seams with every move. "Think nothing of it. I always like to serve my faithful customers with special care."

Zuri started toward the ship's open bay door. He stopped and turned around. "Just one little question."

Uv's bulbous blue eyes blinked in innocence. "Yes?"

"Just outta curiosity—where'd you find it?" He shifted the tube further back on his square shoulder. "I looked everywhere."

Uv's thick lips wobbled in a perky grin. "Well, normally, I don't give away my secrets—but you're one of a kind, Zuri. I don't mind being like clear water with you." He glanced aside.

Two Crestas consulted a console to the right and spoke in low murmurs.

Twitching Zuri's arm, Uv motioned him closer to the bay door. They stopped at a large color-coated map of their sector. Uv tapped a section on the left. "You can't see it, but there's a speck here that's quite valuable. A tiny system in what they call the Milky Way." He shuddered. "Don't ask me what they were thinking. Disgusting name."

Zuri frowned and leaned in. "You mean Earth? I've been there. Barbaric. Full of wild animals and wilder people."

Uv's eyes widened. "When were you there?"

"Centuries ago." Zuri patted his chest. "I've had almost all new parts put in since then."

Uv pursed his lips. "Looks like you might need a few more soon." He shook himself. "Well, anyway, they've gotten past the crust...put primitive vessels into space...and dropped parts along the way."

Zuri tilted his head, his gaze swerving to the object on his shoulder, his eyebrows arching. "This comes from—"

"We had to make alterations to make the blasted thing useful. But, as far as raw parts are concerned, Earth is a fertile field." His lips puffed into a smile. "Crestas make the most of every situation."

Zuri thrust out his own chest. "Ingots are famous for resourcefulness." He turned and strutted toward the door. "I'll have to make a return visit to that planet." He waved and chuckled. "Never know what a little speck might offer."

Live With That

Originally published on The Writings of A. K. Frailey
8/31/2018

—OldEarth—

If Tally hadn't been so frightened, she would've screamed. Without a coherent thought, she backed up, on tiptoes. One step. Two steps.

The huge, bright-colored snake lifted its head, its beady eyes staring right at her. Its wiggly tongue flickered out and in.

A quick glance, right and left, told Tally that no one could rescue her. Slowly, she took another step backward.

A faint peep behind her set her heart racing. Turning her head, she glanced from a baby bird and its broken nest back to the snake. Her stomach churned.

The snack sashayed to the left, arching its body; its beady eyes fixed on the baby bird.

A choking sob clutched Tally's throat; tears started in her eyes. *No.*

The little bird hopped forward, unaware, cheeping innocently. Two grown birds fluttered to a nearby branch, squawking uproariously.

With a flash of red, the snake darted forward.

The parent birds screeched. The baby bird hopped madly.

"No!" Tally grabbed a rock, flung it at the snake's head, turned and scooped the bird into her arms. She pelted away, the little bird fluttering in her fingers, her heart thudding against her chest. Scrambling up a tree, she nestled the baby bird in a wide crook and scampered down again. The parent birds flew near and scolded her.

Pounding steps turned her attention. Liam, her older brother, jogged toward her. "You hurt?"

Tally swallowed and gulped down heaving sobs. She pointed to the snake. "It wanted to kill the bird—but I saved it."

Liam frowned at the sight of a red tail slithering under a bush by the creek. Liam's frown darkened. "We can't have him roaming around." He glanced back to the house. "You go inside. I'll take care of him."

Tally glanced up. The parent birds were on the branch right above the baby bird.

Her brother's gaze followed hers. "They'll be all right. Birds know what to do."

Tally turned to her brother. "Do they?" A sinking feeling etched a hole in her stomach. "I saved it today—but what about tomorrow?" She glanced at the woods and all the fluttering wings among the branches. "How about when I'm not here?"

Her brother's gaze softened. He put his arm around his little sister's shoulder. "You can't save everyone." He shrugged. "Even snakes gotta eat."

"Do they?"

"To keep the natural balance. It's how the world works."

Tally shrugged off her brother's arm and faced the house.

Liam frowned at her. "You okay? It didn't bite you?"

Tally shuffled toward her home. "It didn't bite, but it's like I got poisoned anyway." She glanced at three huddled birds. "At least that one will see another day." She met her brother's somber gaze. "I'll have to live with that."

—Planet Helm—

Bhuaci Village

Dressed in a long, yellow nightdress, Yana tucked her pixie-looking little girl into a swaying hammock hanging from stout beams crisscrossing the ceiling. "You have a good time today? The Kazan zoo is world renowned."

The child nodded and clutched a pink blanket close to her chest. "But the guide said that some animals have gone extinct. We'll never see them again."

Yana gazed into her child's luminous blue eyes. "It's true, I'm afraid. There's a season for everything."

"Will we go extinct?"

Yana's eyes filled with tears. "There are not many of us left." She shook her head. "We fall victim to trials and treachery from within...and without."

"But couldn't we just leave—go somewhere else where no one will bother us?"

Yana smoothed her daughter's furrowed brow. "Survival is more than keeping the body alive—it means keeping the spirit alive as well. That is our greatest danger. We succumb to despair."

"Then we must hope to live."

Tears filled Yana's eyes. "We have seen too much. Suffered too deeply."

"But I haven't. I believe…we'll live forever."

Yana paused, her hand hovering over her daughter's clenched fist. She brushed away a tear. "Perhaps you have the antidote to the poison in our world. To hope—even beyond despair."

A Tie That Can't Be Broken

Originally published on The Writings of A. K. Frailey
9/14/2018

—OldEarth—

Cerulean, a Luxonian dressed in casual twentieth-century blue jeans, a loose t-shirt, and slip-on shoes (he hated laces), rolled a shopping cart along the grocery aisle, following a woman and her young daughter.

The woman, distracted and hesitant, returned repeatedly to the child. "What's next, Anne?"

Holding a limp notepaper covered in careful script, Anne ran her finger along a middle line and bit her lip. She peered at her mom. "Mayonnaise and garlic salt."

The older woman started forward, peered at three varieties of mayonnaise, and froze. The child stepped around her, considered the labels, and plucked the middle choice off the shelf. "It's what we always get."

The woman nodded.

After dropping a box of granola bars and a can of olives into his cart, Cerulean followed, fascinated by the mother and daughter before him. Only when a middle-aged man stared pointedly at his nearly empty cart, did he grab a few more items and toss them in with the others.

The child's preternatural competence struck Cerulean like a blow to the chest. His mother died when he was young, not an uncommon experience for Luxonians. But his memories included a woman of great sensitivity and quiet competence. Nothing like this fragile, hesitant woman pacing behind her strong-willed child.

When they left the store, Cerulean half expected the child to slip into the driver's seat, but no, the older woman took the wheel and ever-so-slowly drove away. Placing his paid-for groceries next to a homeless man he has noticed earlier, Cerulean stepped into a sheltered corner and disappeared.

—Planet Lux—

Cerulean marched into Judge Sterling's quarters, handed his tasty Earth offering to his superior, stepped back, and waited.

Sterling, in his usual gray leggings and a long tunic, grinned and daintily peeled the orange foil away from a sticky granola bar. He eyed it, sniffed it, and then delicately bit off a tiny corner. He chewed, his gaze rising to the bright skylight. "Hmmm. Not bad. Certainly not as disgusting as some of the things your father brought home."

Folding his arms over his chest, Cerulean maintained a steady gaze. "He told me that you had a particular taste for OldEarth brews."

Waving a finger, Sterling cracked a grin. "Teal had a rare knack for highlighting my weak spots." He laid the remainder of the chewy bar on his desk and circled around to an open window with a large garden box attached to the edge.

A luxurious purple vine spread thick along the border and up the walls. Delicate pink flowers dotted the vine clusters creating an enchanting, almost luminescent contrast.

221

"You know, your father gave me this plant many seasons ago. I nearly killed it—accidentally of course. But he saved it. Like he saved so many."

Cerulean shrugged. "Yet you never liked him."

Teal twirled around, the edges of his eyes glowing a fiery red. "I loved your father as few ever could. Even your mother, bless her departed spirit, never really understood him."

Strolling to the plant, Cerulean gently ran his fingers along the main stem, his gaze focused, his heart aching. "What did you understand?"

"Teal was a savior-type. Couldn't help himself. He had to save everyone. Even beings that didn't deserve his...devotion."

"And that was wrong?"

Sterling pursed his lips. "Not wrong exactly— just made my job rather difficult." He stepped closer to Cerulean and clasped his arm. "Do you have any idea how hard it is to keep a savior alive?"

Cerulean locked eyes with Sterling. "Since he's dead now, I can only assume it was an impossible task."

Sterling closed his eyes and swayed back to his desk, landing on a plush chair. With a groan, he propped his head on one hand and stared at Cerulean, who still stood by the plant. "Don't blame me, Cerulean. You know perfectly well I tried to talk him out of going...but—" His sigh rose high and strangled. "You know your father."

Cerulean lowered his gaze, his shoulders dropping, his spirit caving. "Yes. He was certainly determined."

Sterling jumped to his feet, rubbing his hands like a man ready to change the topic if not the world. "So, tell me. Have you chosen a human to focus on?"

Pulling a datapad from a pocket, Cerulean strode to the desk, tapped the surface, and then laid it on the desk.

The picture of a young girl standing next to a slump-shouldered, gray-haired woman peered up.

Cerulean pointed. "Her name is Anne Smith. She's only seven, but—" His gaze wandered across the room, over the vine, and out the window. "I don't know. She seems to have an unusual strength of character. I'd like to see what life has in store for her and how she handles it."

Sterling lifted the datapad and stared at the figures for a long moment. Then he glanced at Cerulean and handed it back. "Don't get emotionally attached."

"Being that she's a human child and I'm a Luxonian adult, I hardly think that'll be an issue."

Sterling nodded through a snort. His eyes grew wide as he lifted the melted chewy bar and strands of caramel and chocolate dribbled across his desk. He swallowed and shook his head. "When are you going?"

"Tomorrow. I thought I'd visit my parents' tombstones before I go."

Sterling tossed the remainder of the bar into a wall depository, snatched a cloth off a shelf, and wiped his hands. "Odd practice. They've departed to the other side, yet you insist on raising a memorial. Why?"

"Parents and children—it's a tie that can't be broken."

Sterling strode over to the purple plant, tugged a young vine free, roots and all, and placed it into Cerulean's open palm. "Plant it between them." He glanced up, and though he smiled, his eyes glinted in grief. "Remember to water it."

Cerulean nodded and started for the door. Then he stopped and glanced back. "Though my father crossed a line—he cared too much—he didn't care alone. Did he?"

Sterling swallowed and dropped his gaze.

Cerulean stepped over the threshold, and the door swished shut.

Alive and Willful

Originally published on The Writings of A. K. Frailey
7/31/2020

—Newearth—

Like all Ingots, Lang's body from the neck down was encased in techno-armor, but her form-fitting suit outlined the fantasies of multiple beings.

She peered at the photo and had to ask—"Was I ever young?"

Riko, a slim Uanyi, could not say. He sat behind his desk with three saucepans lined up along the edge, a large datapad front and center, a holograph pad on the left, and a half-eaten slice of carrot cake on the right. Two baskets of colorful plants hung in front of a large window that now only reflected the outside security light.

Lang laid the photo on Riko's desk and stared pointedly at the pots. "You keep your kitchen utensils close at hand, eh?"

With a shrug, Riko stood and strolled over to a small cooler unit. "I'm ordering new. Wendell tries, but the kid is hard on kitchenware."

"I thought he just worked the tables."

"He only has to look at a pot and it falls to the ground, dents, cracks to pieces...I don't know. It's like the kid has a magnetic storm following him everywhere he goes."

Lang shrugged. "He was a reject that his mama saved. Few Ingots get through infancy—"

Riko hauled two cold drinks out of the cooler, snapped them open, and handed one to Lang.

Lang eyed the bright blue drink and grinned. "Thanks. I was feeling a little parched."

"How about you?" Riko snapped up the photo. "This is old. Somebody treasured it. Most people only have digital memories." One eyebrow rose. "Especially Ingots."

Lang took a long swallow and leaned on the back of a dark brown office couch. "I was a reject too. You'd be surprised how many of us there are. In my case, I was borderline, and because I had a pretty face, they let me through. Never knew my mama or daddy's DNA. That's why Wendell is so different. His mama should never have known. She must've been from one of those back-to-nature groups. They practically stripped themselves naked, then tried to raise their young the old way."

"But someone took this—" Riko waved the photo and took a swig from the bottle.

"Wasn't any family relation—"

A knock on the door turned their attention.

Another quick drink and Riko strode over and swung open his office door.

Wendell stood in the hall between the café kitchen and the office, sheepish but smiling. "I fixed sink. Everything all cleaned up."

Riko nodded. "Good." He jogged to his desk and swiped one of the pots from the line. "Give your ma this. I decided to go with another set, so she can use it. No point in throwing it out."

Wendell accepted the pot, cuddling it in both arms, a grateful servant of a kind benefactor.

Riko shuffled his feet, awkward kindness hindering his usual impatience. "You can go home now. See you in the morning."

Reciting from memory, Wendell raised his eyes to the ceiling and pointed emphatically, his voice imitating Riko's command tone. "Bright and early!"

The two grinned at each other.

The depth of the shared moment almost broke Lang's heart. As Riko closed the door, still grinning, Lang lifted the photo again. "So tell me again—how'd you get this?"

"It was on my desk this morning." He took a final swig, wiped his lips, and met Lang's stare. "Either someone is having a little fun with us, or we'd better keep our eyes open."

Lang drained the last of the blue liquid. "Maybe both." She shrugged. "But as a reporter, I'd sure like to know who—" With a staggering step, Lang fell onto the couch. "Oh, God!"

Riko ran to her side, his eyes wide, frightened. "What?"

"There was a man...he looked like a man. But now...I wonder." She dropped her head in her hands, her gaze roving to Riko's face. "Do you believe in the supernatural?"

Riko choked. He yanked open the recycle depository and tossed in the two empty bottles. "I believe there's more to the universe than we see or understand if that's what you mean."

A tumble of emotions swirled through Lang's system. "I mean an intentional being—beings. Alive and willful."

"Like Omega?"

"Could be...but more." Lang rose; logic overthrowing confusion. "Like the fact that you and I met, that Faye and Taug are buddies, that Cerulean even exists...the million and one oddities, proving that more than mere chance defines out fate."

Riko dropped onto the couch wearily. "You asked if you'd ever been young...well, I grew up in a war zone; my ma was killed trying to protect a way of life that no longer existed, and I certainly never felt young." He met Lang's eyes. "Never."

Lang plunked down next to Riko, their shoulders touching. "Me neither. I was plucked out of the Ingot world by some unknown hand and trained as a reporter before my synapses were set. My body has always been my biggest asset, but collected nerves saved my life. Yet, I've always felt sad."

In uncharacteristic generosity and intimacy, Riko clasped Lang's hand. "Me too."

For a moment, Lang felt young again.

Not Sad

Originally published on The Writings of A. K. Frailey
8/28/2020

—Newearth—

Riko couldn't believe his eyes. His nostrils or his ears either, for that matter. He stared at the gray-walled room filled with bassinets, child-sized beds, and three full-sized beds and promptly slipped into shock.

The cacophony of sounds smashed against his ears like an out-of-tune orchestra that has no intention of ever playing the same composition—each rising burst out-screaming, crying, whimpering, or wailing every other.

The stink gagged him. He pressed his hand to his nostrils and swallowed back bile. *This is literally a shitty situation.*

He tried to count the babies kicking their arms and legs, the tiny pale faces peering over the edge of their bed rails, and the little bodies running in circles in the center of the room, but dizziness engulfed him.

One teenager stood in the center of the room while the little ones ran circles around him gleefully. He waved his hand like a conductor and grinned, apparently unconcerned that madness reigned.

A middle-aged woman bustled forward, her hands extended. "You must be Riko!"

Nodding, unable to take his eyes off the insane circus, Riko merely assented to the truth of the statement.

"I'm Marge. Shwen told me all about you. I'm so glad you've come."

Dragging his attention off the children, Riko peered at the woman. "Shwen?"

"She's a Bhuaci healer. One of the best, if reports are true. Word of you met her ears, and she passed the information to me."

With a shiver, Riko managed to focus on Marge. "I don't understand. Why am I here?"

A screaming boy yanked his attention across the room. A short, buxom woman hurried over and swooped the distraught child into her arms, rocking him with all the force of a turbo engine at high speed.

Marge tapped Riko's arm. "Come with me, and we can talk privately."

Struggling against rising nausea, Riko marched after the matronly figure.

They exited the one-story building through a red back doorway and entered a lovely garden surrounded by multicolored rose bushes, flowering trees, and a tall, woven fence.

Marge led the way to a wooden bench and sat, heaving a relieved sigh. "Lord, have mercy. This is the first time I've been able to rest today." A gentle, depreciating smile wavered on her lips. "I'm really too old to be a mother to such a brood, but someone has to love them."

Riko shook his head. "Where do they come from?"

Marge shrugged. "Everywhere. And nowhere. At least no one will admit to their existence. Some are Ingot rejects. Others were lost in transport and forgotten."

"They're all Ingots then?"

"Not all, but most, yes. A few humans among the lot."

"I didn't see any techno-armor—"

"Most never had the implants, or those that did, didn't adjust well. In any case, we have them now, and we're trying to manage as best we can without such barbaric advancements."

Despite the ironic humor, weary depression settled over Riko. "Why isn't the Inter-Alien Alliance helping you?"

Leaning back, resting her hands in her lap, Marge looked into the sky and snorted. "*No one* wants them. The Inter-Alien Alliance has enough to manage without dealing with unwanted babies." She shrugged.

Apprehension needled Riko. "But you asked me to come today—?"

Taking a deep breath, Marge sat up and slapped her hands on her thighs. "Yes. I have one Ingot teen that needs special assistance. Clearly, he is too old to stay here, but he's not ready to move on his own." She stood and started to stroll the parameter of the enclosed garden. "I found a good woman who is willing to take him in, provided that he finds gainful employment. She's struggling to raise her own three after her husband was killed in a transport accident."

Riko fell in step beside Marge and thought back to the room with the teen standing in the center. "You mean the boy—"

"His name is Wendell. We don't know much about him, where he has been, or how he found us. He just showed up at the door one day looking lost and confused." Marge stopped and laid her hand on Riko's arm as if to emphasize her point.

"But he never looked or acted pitifully. He has complied with everything we've asked. He was the one who started the children running in circles around him every day."

Riko reared back. "Does that help?"

"Yes, marvelously! They are so much calmer after they've had a good run. I bring them out here sometimes but only in small groups, or they'd tear this place to shreds. They are still a bit out of control." She sighed and reconvened her stroll.

Riko stroked his chin, pondering the question he knew was coming. How could he say yes? But more importantly, how could he say no? The datapad on his wrist chimed, alerting him to the lateness of the hour. He stopped. "Can we go back in?"

Marge nodded, solemn and silent.

This time the noise and smell didn't shock him as it had at first. Either it wasn't as bad as he had imagined, or he was getting used to it. He hoped he wasn't getting used to it.

Wendell stood leaning over one of the beds. He covered and uncovered parts of his face in a rhythmic pattern.

Perplexed, Riko strode closer.

The child in the bed grinned as she imitated Wendell's every move. When he covered his eyes, she covered hers, at least partially. One eye peeked out, watching for the next step. When he covered his nose, she did the same, giggling.

A lump formed in Riko's throat. He stepped up and laid his hand on Wendell's shoulder. "I hear that you're looking for a job."

After patting the little girl's head, Wendell turned his attention to Riko. "Need work for the new mom." He smiled, innocence incarnate.

With an inward groan, Riko thrust his hand out. "I happen to be looking for a boy to help me at the café."

Wendell stared at Riko's outstretched hand and tilted his head, perplexed.

Sighing, Riko grabbed Wendell's hand and shook it. "It's a human expression, a way of sealing a deal. You'll work with me at the Breakfastnook, starting tomorrow. That way your new mom can rest easy, and you can get out of this madhouse."

"Madhouse?" Wendell glanced around. "Not mad. Only sad."

For the first time since his mother died, Riko blinked back tears. "Yeah, well, you'll come early, okay? Marge will give you directions. It's not far."

Wendell grinned. "I go there. Tomorrow. Work early. Come here. Run kids. Not sad."

Swallowing the urge to sob like one of the babies, Riko nodded and cleared his throat. "A good plan." He turned and hustled to Marge's side as she placed a baby in a high chair with a plastic bowl filled with bright-colored cereal.

"I expect him bright and early in the morning."

Peering through exhausted eyes, Marge smiled. "Thank you."

Riko turned and fled out the doorway.

Once safely back at the café, Riko threw himself into the bustling dinner crowd as they ate and chattered, making a pleasant raucous.

He thought back to the orphanage. Funny, but he couldn't recall the noise or the stink. Only the smiles. Not sad at all.

Vacation Paradise

Originally published on *Bad Science Fiction Read Poorly* ~By Dick and Jay
https://anchor.fm/bsfrp/episodes/Hazard-Pay–with-Special-Guest-A–K–Frailey-Overexposure—Vacation-Paradise—The-Solar-Pump-Archipelago-elt2m7
Then published on The Writings of A. K. Frailey
12/22/2020

Sven massaged the woman's flesh with renewed vigor. His last day! Visions of vacation paradise floated before his eyes.

A groan froze his fingers. Oops! He peered down at the figure sprawled on the table under his skilled hands. Perhaps the warm-up massage was a bit much for her first time.

Sliding off the edge of middle age, Ms. Tolliver had stumbled into his office last week, complaining about shoulder and neck pain. He had done a quick check, diagnosed the problem—frozen shoulder undoubtedly—lots of ladies her age suffered from the common ailment, and set up a schedule for Physical Therapy three times a week for three weeks. He only had to manage the first visit, and then, while he was gone—having the time of his life—his aides would take over. By the time he returned, she'd be ready to beat her university peers at a high stakes game of Zinzinera.

Sven frowned as he stared at her. She didn't look very good at the moment. Her color seemed off somehow. Granted lots of ladies liked to dye their skin all sorts of weird colors these days. The multi-colored zebra look rather turned his stomach, but hey, who was he to make fashion comments. It was the year 4798 after all, and humanity knew how to have fun...

Speaking of fun...his mind trailed away to the playground he was going to enjoy for twenty whole days.

After the designated warming pad to relax the stretched tendons, Sven handed Ms. Tolliver a list of twelve routine exercises she could practice at home.

She wrinkled her nose, peering at the datapad as if she wasn't sure what it all meant.

Annoyance crept over Sven. Good golly, was she an idiot? "They're the same exercises I just did with you. Just repeat them at home each day and come in on your scheduled visits. You'll be good as new in no time."

Doubt clouded her eyes.

Fury boiled up in Sven. She doubts me? *Me?* Why, I'm the best physical therapist on the entire island. He had won the Australian "Healthy Lives" award six years running. Six! Bloody idiot. She didn't deserve his attention. Just as well that he'd leave her to his aides. They weren't as good as he was...well, that hardly mattered. They were good enough. He had trained them, after all. NewContinetalEurpose wanted him to speak at their next Inter-Alien symposium on how physical therapy could assist communication in mixed marriages. A bit of a stretch in his mind—after all, physical therapy wasn't a cure-all. But heck, who was he to refuse the honor?

Ms. Tolliver tapped his arm. "Sorry, but I'm not sure I understand. I mean, I don't think I can—"

A bell chimed.

Closing time!

Sven's heart pounded in anticipation while his voice rose above the tumult of various therapists, aides, and clients preparing to leave for the day. "You'll be just fine! Go home, put your feet up, and relax." He didn't exactly mean to nudge her toward the door, but the silly idiot didn't seem to realize that it was time to go.

In a matter of minutes, he had loaded his packed bags on the transport and was heading off planet to his dream vacation. He deserved some fun. After all, he worked hard and no one knew how to thank Sven better than he did.

Three weeks later...

Chenier grabbed a bottle of polish and tried once again to wipe the blood spot off her uniform. It wasn't a big spot, but part of it smeared her embroidered nametag—Chenier Dobson, Physical Therapist Aide. Marcus had one just like it, except of course, his stated his name, Marcus Arius, and there was no blood spot on his. He had kept his distance when the poor woman started to bleed out.

Chenier sighed. She didn't regret her actions. There was little she could have done to change the outcome. But she did think her boss had been a little remiss. In fact, he had bungled the whole affair. Complete records were due on her datapad by the end of the day. Perhaps they would give her a better idea of what had really happened.

The chime signaled the start of a new day. She glanced at the roster streamed to the wallboard. A full week of patients waiting for relief from pain.

Marcus trotted near and leaned in, whispering, "He's back."

Fear shivered down Chenier's spine. "Does he know, you think?"

"Not by the look on his face." Marcus sneered. "He's been having the time of his life. His mother could've died, and he'd probably shrug it off."

Chenier frowned. "His mother died seven years ago and, from the records, he doesn't have much to do with his DNA relations."

Marcus heaved a sigh and pressed his colleague's shoulder. "Don't expect too much." He glanced at the line of men and women shuffling into the room. "It's our job to relieve pain and loosen up tight joints. No one could've known Ms. Tolliver's condition. She never said anything. So, let it go. Don't even bother telling him. He won't care."

Chenier bit her lip as she watched her friend stride away.

Sven sauntered near, raising one hand in languid salute. "So, how are things? I've had the best vacation of my life!"

Chenier nodded. She squinted. Something seemed off about his color. A tinge green, perhaps? She shrugged the thought away. "You had a good time, I take it."

"Of all the playgrounds off-planet, Corpus is the absolute best. I've already made reservations to go back next season." He wiggled his eyebrows. "Can't get too much of a good thing, I always say." He looked around. "Everything as I left it?"

Chenier braced herself. "Well, there was one case, Ms. Tolliver..."

Sven yawned and stretched. "I need a little PT myself. Been having a bit of pain in my shoulder." He rubbed his neck. "It got a little vigorous at one point..." He grinned. "If you know what I mean."

Chenier stuck to her point like plaster to the wall. "Ms. Tolliver died on her third visit. Apparently, she suffered from—"

"That old biddy? She couldn't follow directions if there were written on her synapsis. Don't worry about it." Alarm spread across his face. "Unless someone here—"

"No, it wasn't our fault. It's just that she had a pre-existing condition. She had—"

"Oh, well, then. Forget it. As long as it wasn't out fault. I mean, old women die. Happens all the time. We're Physical Therapists. We're not God. Can't fix everyone, you know." He smiled down at his well-trained aide. "Just get on with your work." He rolled his shoulders. "I'll get Marcus to give me a bit of a work out. Gosh but I'm feeling a stiff today."

Chenier watched him stumble across the padded floor, his arms stiffly at his side. "Serves him right if he does have a pulled joint or two." She shrugged, checked the roster, and called on her first patient.

~~~

A week later, Chenier stood before the open vault, tapping her fingers against her thigh. She

239

hated this place. Sweat dripped down her back, and she remembered with chagrin that she'd forgotten her deodorant this morning. Of all days too. Fear stank, and she was always afraid at these things.

When Marcus strolled up, relief surged through her. "Thank, God. I was thinking you might not show."

Marcus held up his datapad. "I'm designated secretary. The Inter-Alien Alliance wants a record. Apparently, this is now considered a dangerous trend." He smirked. "Guess there is such a thing as having too much fun."

Chenier pouted. "Ms. Tolliver didn't do anything wrong. She just didn't think to mention that she had just come back from vacation. Who would?"

Marcus lifted his hand authoritatively. "Sven should've seen the signs..."

With a sigh, Chenier shook her head. "If he had cared to see the danger for her, he might've seen it for himself. Funny that."

Marcus snorted. "Yeah, well, once I get his remains sent off, I'm taking a vacation myself."

Chenier's eyes widened. "Where to?"

Marcus laughed. "Me? Oh, I'm just going home to spend time with my DNA relations. As for Sven's remains? Well, I'm sending them to Vacation Paradise. It's where he always wanted to be."

No Glaciers Needed

Originally published on The Writings of A. K. Frailey
2/16/2021

—Planet Lux—

Chasm stood on the baked and pounded ground and stared at his shoes, profoundly aware that they were several sizes larger than the others lined up beside his. A cool breeze cascaded over his hot body. He could hear his mother's words loud and clear. "Don't get overheated, boyo, 'cause I can't find any glaciers to cool you off this time of year."

He forced his smile in check.

The kid next to him squirmed.

Chasm nudged him. "Don't move, Oleg, or he'll kill us."

The boy heaved a strained, exasperated sigh.

Coach screamed, "Hey, you two! Give me five more!"

Oleg's eyes widened with horror.

Chasm choked. "Wasn't my fault!"

The twenty-eight boys held the line, observing in constrained silence as Chasm awkwardly led the smaller boy around the track, taking tiny steps to keep pace with his companion's short strides.

Giggles broke the tense silence.

Coach, his arms crossed high over his barrel chest, stood on the sidelines grinning, his jaws masticating contraband chewing gum.

The blazing Luxonian sun seethed in a white sky, heat piercing through protective covering.

Even the best eye protection was a poor defense against the damaging rays.

A wonder more of us don't go blind. Chasm wiped sweat off his brow as he jogged forward, his arms limp at his side. *Three more...*

Oleg stumbled.

Chasm reached out.

The boy fell limply in his arms.

"Drop him and finish your laps!" Clearly, Coach enjoyed his work.

The watching boys froze, stiff as petrified rocks.

So many times, he'd come home burning with humiliation, a sorry excuse for a son, but his mother's nudge combined with a healthy snort, always revived his drooping spirits. "Think you got it rough? Try being a giant woman! Then you'd know what rough looked like up close and personal. Giant guys are fine. But giant gals scare the hell out of most everybody, even Luxonian shapeshifter-types. Lordy, they can morph into Ingoti Lava Lizards, but a seven-foot human woman sets 'em giggling in weird ways." Her black eyes flashed, and her ebony skin glistened as she jutted her chin, contempt oozing through every pour. Until a glint of humor discharged the poison. "Should thank their lucky suns I'm so good-natured, or they might not be so powerful now."

Chasm knew the story, oft-repeated, how she managed to chase off a strange ship that landed in one of the busiest intersections of the capitol. No one knew who the aliens were or why they'd come. But the Luxonian crowd that gathered round had been profoundly grateful for Adah's help. Unexpected as it was.

Oleg groaned.

Being the only refugee over seven feet tall, many boys looked to him for help. Chasm didn't mind, but he wasn't sure what to do most of the time. He looked around for help.

Coach sauntered forward. Unlike most Luxonians, his attitude sparked with resentment at the outsiders. Even though the human refugees had originally come to Lux by invitation, coach narrowed his eyes at every specimen he met, especially the boys he forced out under the sun "to keep them fit and healthy" as his job description decreed.

Killing us with kindness.

Chasm gripped Oleg's limp body tighter.

Rex, a lanky kid, not nearly Chasm's size but with an outsized spirit that towered above the average, stepped from the disciplined line. "We're done here."

Coach turned his full glare on Rex's impassive, staring eyes. "You think so?"

Rex nodded.

"How about I make you all do ten more?"

Rex peered along the line of watching boys.

Everyone knew that they lived at the mercy of their hosts—Luxonians who had accepted the burden of caring for a dying race of beings—but resentment had elbowed its way in over the years, making humans not so welcome.

Chasm's heart clenched as his gaze darted from Rex to Oleg's reviving form.

Oleg shook himself free and stood on shaky legs. He blinked as he stared at the coach. "Think you can kill me?"

Coach's amused glance spoke volumes.

Rex waved at the line of boys ahead with a formal bow. "He can try. But we don't have to let him." He sauntered off the track.

The line wavered, eyes following but feet still.

Oleg gripped Chasm's arm. "Let's go." He strode after Rex, panting but determined.

As the sound of footsteps padded after them, Chasm's heart swelled. No matter his size, he finally filled his shoes. No glaciers needed.

To Make a Difference
Science Fiction Novella

Originally published on The Writings of A. K. Frailey
3/17/2017

Soul-Searing

Autumn is always bittersweet and beautiful—like a memory. I am nearly fifty now and yet my childhood seems as close as the doorway. More distant, and more painful are the memories of my sons. I had only two, Joseph and David, both fine young men, each born with a high sense of duty. One is dead, and the other might be soon. People tell me that I can't change anything—that fate is what it must be. I try to accept that. But the memories haunt me, like autumn. They beguile me with their sweetness and then frighten me with what comes after.

I grew up endowed with a mission to change the world. I was going to *be somebody*. My relations going all the way back to Adam and Eve were much the same. It must be something in our genetic code. We were the branch that reached for the sun and was never content to live in the shade of another's glory. My father was a radio broadcaster, and my mother was an artist. They both strove with straining hearts to be great at what they did. You probably never heard of them. Few ever did. But they lived and died believing that they made a difference. And I guess that is all that really matters, believing in yourself. At least, that is what David keeps telling me.

It is late now, and the house is quiet. The cicada came out late this year, and I can still hear them in the evenings joining their songs with the crickets and the frogs. It makes a low, pleasant hum, always in the background, like the music in a movie. You aren't always aware of it, but it affects your mood and soothes or warns you, as the case may be. Right now, the evening sounds are soothing. There are no dreadful winds screeching against the windows or thunder hammering on the roof. Right now, I feel peaceful and even a little drowsy. David should be home soon. His shift ended at 8:00 P.M., but he said it might take him a little longer as he was going to talk to his director about his options. That is what he calls it, *his options.*

War broke out again four years ago, and I thought that Joseph would stay out of it, but since he was trained as a psychiatric nurse, he saw it as his duty to join up as soon as possible and help out in whatever way he could. I admired his patriotism. Everyone did. After all, we had not looked for war. It came to us, landed in our laps when extremist terrorists set off bombs in our cities. There have always been problems in the world and tensions were especially high with threats at the time, but I had always figured that we were secure, our lives would remain on the periphery of events. I had hoped that living in the countryside might shield us. But fate crosses all boundaries and Joseph was determined to make a difference. He wanted to save people. He wanted to be helpful. How could I blame him? Over a thousand people were killed in those attacks and more died in the following battles. War comes at a cost. But I hoped that it would not cost the life of my son. I am not sure why I thought he should be exempt. But I did. I honestly thought that he was too good to die.

So now I sit here trying to make sense of my memories and trying to decide what I believe. If fate rules us, then it really does not matter what I believe. I can sit here until Doom's Day, and nothing will change. But if fate is just an excuse for not accepting our part of things, then perhaps it does matter. Maybe I have more to do with Joe's death than I realize. Maybe David still has a chance.

~ ~ ~

Kurt and I were older when we got married. It took us a long time to find each other. We were like that song— "Looking for love in all the wrong places." But eventually, we met right where you'd expect two Catholics might meet, in a church. It was at Christmas time, and we were both out of college, and it turned out we had some friends in common. It didn't take us long to decide that we wanted a life together. It did take a couple years to pay off old debts and clear out our lives so that we could make room for our marriage. But once that was taken care of, we went forward and had a big wedding, inviting everyone near and far. We're both believers but not terribly involved in church activities, except around holiday time. Our lives revolved more around our work. I had been endowed with a missionary spirit, teaching in poor neighborhoods while Kurt had worked as an English as a Second Language instructor. Both of us were zealots. Both of us wanted to make a difference. And both of us were rather tired and worn out by the time we got married.

It took us three years to have our first child, but there was never a more anticipated bundle of joy than out little Joe. Suddenly all our zeal was directed toward this tiny little baby. It was as if no other baby had ever been born before, the way we acted. Kurt made every birthday a major holiday and started to teach little Joe the letters of the alphabet and how to play ball when he was barely old enough to toddle across the floor.

I was intent on providing the best home and the nicest, most delicious meals ever created by any mother anywhere. The poor child never had a chance to know moderation. Moderation just wasn't in our vocabulary. If he even got a sniffle, I ran him to the pediatrician so fast that the doctor would usually just tell me to turn around and go home, giving me nothing more than an encouraging word and a slight sigh. Joseph either had a great immune system or we frightened every illness away before it had a chance for Joe grew up as healthy as an ox. He grew big too. The other kids in school used to say that he ought to try out for football, but I'd never let him. It was too risky. He had a smart mind, and I didn't want his head broken in some game that would only decide the fate of a team for a season. I wanted my boy to make decisions about far more important things. Luckily Kurt agreed with me. Kurt would read him stories by the hour about famous men in history. That boy went to bed dreaming about knights in shining armor and martyrs who suffered for their faith. Though we lived in farm country and envied farmers their knack for bringing fruit from the earth, even if it was simply acres and acres of corn or beans, still we never saw ourselves as farmer types. We had the missionary spirit. So, when Joe grew up and chose medicine as his field, Kurt and I smiled in complete understanding. This was something worthy, something grand that could make a difference in the world.

Joe joined the Peace Corps after college, and Kurt and I were so proud of him; we could hardly contain ourselves. We sent packages and extra money to support him through the two years he spent in the Philippines. He got Typhoid while he was there, and Kurt thought about going over to check in on him, but Joe told us not to come. His letters became subdued. Joe seemed to be changing in ways I couldn't understand. I wondered if he was depressed, but Kurt said that he was just seeing the world as it really was and that sobered him up a bit. Besides, everyone was telling me: "Joe's his own man now; he's over twenty-one; you need to let him be." It wouldn't do any good to worry anyway. I had no control over the world or my son anymore. There weren't any options I could veto.

When Joe arrived back in the states one blistering hot July day, he met us at the airport looking like an overgrown scarecrow. He had lost so much weight that I barely recognized him. He was tanned, but his face was gaunt with exhaustion. I was appalled, but Kurt gripped my arm and told me not to mother him. He was a man now. Joe needed to tell us what happened in his own way. At least Kurt realized that *something* had happened. But as we drove through the city noise of Saint Louis back toward the rural quiet of Illinois, I waited expectantly for Joe to say something, for him to tell us his story. He didn't.

He hardly talked that whole drive home and he talked very little for the three months that he lived with us before he found a job in Washington D.C. He didn't seem to care about anything except getting busy someplace far away from us. I couldn't understand. I thought my heart might break. I had always considered myself a wonderful mother, but now I wondered what I had done wrong. Why didn't Joe seem to care about me, or his father, or even his little brother? Joe and David had never been especially close but they had been good friends. Now it was as if they hardly knew each other.

David was finishing college, and he was busy with dreams of his own. He seemed grieved by the change in his brother, but he didn't seem inclined to do anything about it. I remember David came to me as I was sitting on the porch watching the sunset one evening and said, "Don't worry about Joe, Mom. He's made his decisions. He can't go back to being your little boy anymore. You've got to accept that."

I had no idea what David was talking about, but it seemed to be the advice everyone was giving me. Even Kurt told me not to worry. Joe was a big boy. He would make his own way. And he did. He made his way right into a psychiatric ward where he was helping men who had returned from the war with serious mental conditions. He was a very capable nurse, and he got along with everyone, well, almost everyone. It was one of his own patients who killed him. Shot him in the heart. I never knew how a patient got ahold of a gun. At the time, it didn't seem to matter. Joe was dead, and that was all I really needed to know.

At his funeral, the director of the hospital came over and shook my and Kurt's hands and tried to console us. He looked me right in the eye and said that Joe died making a difference. I had to believe that was true. But I couldn't understand why it was supposed to make me feel better. After all, if he was making a difference, wouldn't it have been better if he lived? How did his death serve anyone?

It wasn't until Kurt and I were cleaning out Joe's apartment, when I came across his journal that I began to understand the man my son had become. I found the journal tucked under a copy of *The Imitation of Christ* by Thomas A Kempis. I had heard of the book, but I had never read it, and I was surprised to find it among Joe's things. I had been more afraid of finding girlie magazines, but there was none of that. In fact, his whole apartment was rather Spartan. Kurt put a few books in a box and then he said he needed to make some phone calls. He left the room and didn't come back until later that evening when I was about done. I wanted to be angry at him for leaving me to work alone, but then I realized that he couldn't help himself. Kurt wasn't the kind of man who could cry in front of people, even me. He needed to be alone to deal with his grief. I figured pretending that everything was okay was the

251

nicest thing I could do. Sometimes not talking was our way of getting through things.

I gave most of Joe's stuff away, but I kept the journal. I couldn't read it for over a year. But then in late September the following year, I picked it up after lunch, and I didn't put it down even to make dinner. Kurt had gone to a game with some friends, and David was living on campus. I was completely alone. I wish I hadn't been. It was an experience that seared my soul forever.

I've Played My Part

The first part of Joe's journal was much like what I would have expected. He was obsessed with his work, and he wrote about the people he worked with and the things he was doing. But then he wrote about a series of nightmares, which were haunting him and his reflections about what they meant. Then a few entries later, Joe finally admitted that he was struggling with his faith.

There was a time lapse between entries at this point and when he finally started writing again, he wrote about his experiences in the Philippines. He had become good friends with a girl there, and he had even thought about bringing her home and marrying her, but then he discovered that she was pregnant. His friends warned him that he would be in a lot of trouble, so they advised him to help the girl get an abortion. Abortion was not an option for this girl or Joe either, but her father found out, and there was a big scene, and Joe discovered that he was in bigger trouble than he had realized.

The girl's father wanted Joe to marry her right away, and Joe knew that his dreams for the future were seriously compromised. A friend got him some medicine that was supposed to end the pregnancy quick and easy. Joe gave his girlfriend the medication, telling her that it would make everything better. She believed him and took it and soon became so sick she nearly died. The baby miscarried and Joe transferred to another village.

After that, he fulfilled his time in the Peace Corps as perfectly as possible. He wrote that he never even looked at another girl for a long time. He tried to put the whole event out of his mind and promised himself that he would make up for his mistake by being the best nurse he could be. And everything seemed to work out. Except that he couldn't completely forget the girl he once believed he loved, or atone for the past with promises for the future. Nightmares haunted his nights.

I sat there sobbing, hugging Joe's journal, thinking that my son had died a tormented man when I realized that he had left three pages blank before his last entry. When I thought about it later, I realized that perhaps he had left those pages blank for a reason. Maybe he had wanted to mark the place in his journal with white pages, to show the difference in his life. In any case, Kurt came home before I could read that last entry, and it was a long time before I could pick it up again.

Kurt never drank much but occasionally when he was out with friends they would stop by someplace and have a few beers. This particular night, he had had more than a few. I wondered at him as he came in swaying haphazardly and I asked him if he wanted anything to eat, but he just waved me away. He said he had finally realized that his whole life was a sham. He was never any hero, and he had never accomplished anything. The world would be better off without him.

I was shocked and hurt. After all, if his life was a sham, what was mine? What was our marriage? I couldn't understand this pit he had suddenly fallen into, but I did have sense enough to realize that a good night's sleep would probably help, so I pretty much agreed with everything he said, and I helped him to the bedroom. I gave him a back massage and let him mumble himself to sleep.

As I watched him lying obliquely on the bed half-dressed, since I couldn't manage to get him completely undressed or completely straight on the bed, I realized that this was our life. A half-done life. We had the ideals and the zeal, but we didn't have something that made things really work out properly. I wondered about that as I made my way to the living room. I didn't bother undressing either, for I thought Kurt might get sick in the night; he wasn't a drinking man and this little bout with the bottle might have other unpleasant consequences. So I just piled up the couch pillows, and I lay in the dark living room and thought about what I had read in Joe's journal.

I don't know why I didn't just get it and read the last entry, but I felt so overwhelmed that I couldn't take one more emotional revelation. I just lay there and wondered what Kurt had meant by his life being a sham. Was his life really a sham? Didn't he love me? What did that say about my life? I don't know when I fell asleep, but I awoke to the sound of Kurt calling me from the bathroom. There were other unpleasant consequences, all right.

That spring David graduated from college with an engineering degree. He had decided that he wanted to specialize in aeronautics and though I didn't see the "big plan" David seemed to feel that there was one, and he needed to be a part of it. The war had slowed down and was rolling along like many modern wars, mostly on someone else's turf. I read online reports and I wondered if anyone would ever find a way to convince leaders that killing each other's young people was no way to solve our differences. But I could see the necessity of protecting the innocent. After all, "the only way for evil to conquer was for good men to do nothing." I had always believed that. So had Kurt and Joe. But now Kurt was submerged in doubt, and Joe was dead. I had a hard time lifting myself to the heights of idealism that I used to love.

During that spring and early summer, Kurt seemed to be getting ill a lot. He lost weight and looked tired all the time. I urged him to go to see a doctor, but he insisted that it was just a summer cold and he'd get over it. He didn't. By the time he finally did see a doctor, cancer had spread throughout his lymph nodes and into his bones. It had progressed to the point where even the specialists didn't think he had much time left. They were willing to do chemo treatments, but Kurt said that he was too old and too tired to fight that hard. He was ready to go. I couldn't believe what I was hearing. I felt like I never knew my husband at all.

By the fall, Kurt was in the hospital a lot. I would go see him after a full day of teaching and spend the evening with him before I went home to shower and get ready for the next day. As we sat there in that white-walled room, we would sometimes watch TV, or we'd talk about stuff on the news. Kurt always enjoyed discussing current events, and he loved history so he'd often tell me everything he knew about the countries that were in the news. He loved sharing his knowledge. That was one reason he had been such a wonderful ESL teacher. He was smart, and he cared about the people he worked with because he knew something about them and where they came from. He had always seen a connectedness between people and events.

Yet now, as he slowly succumbed to the ravages of cancer, he didn't see himself as being particularly connected to anything or anyone. When I asked him why he was so ready to leave me and David behind, he said, "I'm done—that's all. I played my part and though it wasn't as big as I thought it would be, still, I gave it my all. Now it's my turn to go off stage and let someone else take over."

I remember; I wanted to slap him. I wanted to beat him on the chest and tell him that he wasn't God and no one said he could slip quietly into the dark night. But even as I was shaking with fury, I wondered if I was being fair. Kurt had a right to face his death in his own way, and I should be glad he wasn't suffering any worse. I should be relieved he was accepting his fate. But somewhere in the back of my mind, I was troubled. My heart was hurting and my head was aching. Nothing seemed to be making any sense. I tried to reach back to my youthful sense of high purpose but it was elusive. Everything that used to comfort me was slipping through my fingers. I sat there, the blinds closed against the blazing August sun and Kurt fell into one of his evening naps.

I wondered at my stomach crunching distress. I could feel the familiar ache in my middle and knew that inner turmoil was one of the worst pains in the world. I tried to talk myself out of my suffering. If Kurt was accepting his fate, why couldn't I? If Joe had died making a difference, then what good did it do to grieve over his death? Was I just lonely and frightened? No, I had friends, and I was certainly capable of taking care of myself. Though I was losing my best friend, I didn't need to think I was losing my whole life. My life would still have a purpose. I would still be a valuable person, and I needed to accept what I could not change. But somehow, all my reasoning just made my stomach clench harder and my brain whirl that much faster.

Late one October afternoon, one of Kurt's students came by to see him. He was an elderly Asian man, and though many of Kurt's students had come before to say hi and engage in some kind of humanitarian kindness, this man, I don't even remember his name, was the kindest of all.

He didn't say much, but as Kurt was sleeping, he just came over and shook my hand then he knelt by Kurt's bed and began to pray. I was taken a little aback. I wasn't sure what religion this guy was or who, exactly, he was praying to, but his sincerity was obvious. He stayed there kneeling for what seemed like hours but was probably only just a few minutes. When he got up, he smiled at me and just whispered as he left, "God knows." I have absolutely no idea why those words comforted me so much, but they did. I could actually feel the knots in my middle unloosen a little and though I didn't knee on the floor, I did bow my head.

Certainly, I had prayed for Kurt just like I had prayed for Joe. A priest had come in and anointed Kurt. Our faith had been an intrinsic part of our lives. But suddenly, I saw things from a different view. It was as if I was looking at my life from a new perspective. In my youth, I had always been trying to make a difference. Then as tragedy entered, I tried desperately to grasp its meaning. Everyone advised acceptance but that had seemed cowardly, elusive, a run-away kind of thing. But there, as an October rain drizzled against those never-opened windows, for a brief second, I grasped what I was missing.

Twinkling Stars

Kurt died in November, the day before Thanksgiving. We hadn't planned much since he was so ill but several of his relatives had come to town for family get-togethers so, in a way, it was good timing. Everyone was close, and the funeral was arranged without difficulty. Kurt had insisted on making out a will as soon as he knew he was seriously ill, so money matters slipped into place easily. David came home from his work at NASA, and he did everything he could to help me out. He was as good and kind a son as a mother could want. But he didn't talk much about his work. He just said that there were a lot of wonderful possibilities in the future, and he wanted to explore some of them. I knew he had always been interested in space exploration, but as he turned his attention toward engineering and then toward planes, I figured his childhood fantasies of traveling to far off planets had vanished like other vaporous dreams. It turned out I was wrong.

His dreams had never died and as he faced a world in turmoil and the deaths of his brother and father, his dreams seemed to revive with alacrity. Even during that wet and cold November, he would sit out on the porch in the evenings watching as the sky turned from misty-gray to solemn-black. When I came out and asked him why he didn't come inside where it was warm, he simply said he was watching for any stars which might break through the clouds. I remember telling him that any stars which broke through a November night were more likely to be airplanes or aliens, and he just chuckled and said, "Maybe so, maybe so."

I finally had the courage to read the last chapter of Joe's journal that winter, and I could have kicked myself for waiting so long. It turned out that Joe had met someone in the hospital that he really admired, and he had shared his turmoil with him. The man, whose name was Dr. Scanlon, was just starting out, but he must have had been born with the wisdom of the ages for he told Joe that his mission in life was not defined by his mistakes but by how he handled his mistakes. Apparently, Joe got a new lease on life, and he realized that he would never be a perfect man. That job had already been taken. He was called to be as good a man as he could be, and when he slipped up, he was called to stand up and try again.

I realized as I read this, how commonplace those words seemed. They were the kinds of things I told my fifth graders. But I understood that Joe had grasped them on a whole new level. I suppose someone would say that Joe had been born again. He suddenly seemed to believe that his life had a meaning beyond what he could fully grasp. And that encouraged him. "Thank God," I murmured as I sat there on my bed once more rocking and hugging his journal to my chest. "Thank God."

The next time David came home for a visit, I handed him Joe's journal and told him he'd enjoy the last entry. David only smiled and said that he probably knew more about Joe than I realized. Joe had called him the day before he died and said that he was thinking about asking out a particularly beautiful intern. They had laughed together, and David said he felt that Joe was relieved of a heavy burden. I just stared at my son and asked him if there was any hope that I would know *him* before I died, and he smiled that bewildering smile he has and said that he would share more—if he could. I just sighed and shook my head. David then did one of the most surprising things he has ever done. He took my hand and he led me out to the twilight sky and he pointed to the stars. He said, "Look up there, Mom, and tell me what you see."

I told him I saw a multitude of twinkling lights that scientists tell me are really balls of burning gas bigger than the earth and that though I believe them, I'd be equally content to have them just be twinkling lights. David has such an infectious laugh. I had to laugh with him. We stood there, him holding my hand like a little boy again, and he suddenly turned to me and said, "What if I told you that out there lies the hope of humanity? If only we have the daring to realize it?"

Well, what could I say? What would *you* say? I remembered my youth and I felt a strange flicker of hope and life. I felt his excitement. But I also felt a ripple of fear. What was he about to do? What was he about to risk? I looked at his upturned face and I asked him, "What do you mean? Tell me about it."

David explained. He told me all about how he was working on the design for a settlement on Mars and how one day he hoped to be part of a mission that would initiate the first building efforts on Mars. There was even talk of him being a part of the next space mission so that he could better prepare himself for that experience and have a better understanding of what would be needed for a lifetime in a space settlement. I stared at David, much like I had stared at Kurt, wondering if I ever knew the man in front of me. I asked him why he had never shared these plans with me before, and he chuckled again.

"Some of this is not for the general public, Mom, and besides, it still sounds strange even to my ears. I wasn't sure I could handle the bewildered expression I see in your eyes now. There was a time when I would have doubted my sanity for even dreaming of such things."

"But now?"

David had grinned. "Now I feel confidence born of grace. I trust that if God wants this done, it will be done. And I'll be the man to help do it."

There was so little I could say at that point. I realized that my whole life had been the humus of this dream. David's dream, like so many others: Christopher Columbus, Einstein, Albert Switzer, Mother Teresa, had borne fruit not from the desert of fantasy, but from the nurturing love of family who dared to believe in things, who dared to dream big dreams even when those big dreams ended up being little more than a life well lived or a death well faced. I stood there as the clouds passed away and the stars broke through, twinkling their hearts out. I held my son's hand and I never wanted to let him go.

So, the Earth continues to revolve around the sun in its allotted course, and seven more years have passed. David has been on two space missions, and now, he has to decide if he will go on this last one. This will be a mission that will take him further than even my imagination can travel. He will begin a new phase in his dream. He will be a part of a team that will begin building a settlement on a very, very distant planet. He will likely spend the rest of his life working with robots and men who have sacrificed everything for a home very different from this one. He's never been a coward, and he doesn't expect to start now.

I always wished David would settle down and have a family, but now I see how that was always impossible. He was a man born for a mission. I guess, we all have our missions. Perhaps mine was to give life to such a man and to plant a seed of daring hope.

Have I made a difference? Did Kurt? Surely when Kurt read those stories to the boys, he made a difference in the kind of young men they would be. He did as much as I to form them, not just their bodies, but their very souls. Kurt died believing his mission was over. Joe died trying to help an insane man deal with his suffering, hoping to have a family of his own someday. His life was about never giving up. My mission?

The winds have picked up, and I can hear David's car pull into the driveway. He said he would come home tonight, even if it was late. It's nearly midnight. It is raining now and there is a rumble of thunder in the distance. I suppose, he has accepted his mission.

I suppose I have too.

The forecast says that the temperature will drop tonight, down to the forties. Winter is on its way. Autumn can't last forever. No season ever does. I left some chicken and fixings on a plate for him. I guess I'll warm them up and sit with him awhile. I even made a few chocolate brownies. They're his favorite.

A. K. Frailey

A. K. Frailey has written the historical sci-fi *OldEarth Encounter* series, a contemporary first contact novel, *Last of Her Kind*, the *Newearth* sci-fi series, an *OldTown* series, short story collections, a modern parent's reflection on J. R. R. Tolkien's works in *The Road Goes Ever On: A Christian Journey Through The Lord of the Rings*, personal and introspective *My Road* books, children's books, and a poetry collection.

She taught in Milwaukee, WI, Chicago, IL, Los Angeles, CA, and Wood River, IL, as an elementary education teacher.

She also trained teachers in the Philippines for the Peace Corps and later earned a Master of Fine Arts Degree in Creative Writing for Entertainment from Full Sail University.

Ann homeschooled all her children and currently manages her rural homestead with her family and their numerous critters. In her spare time, she serves as an election judge and secretary/treasurer of her small town's cemetery.

A. K. Frailey Books QR CODES

A. K. Frailey Website

Translated Books Page with Links

A. K. Frailey Interviews Page

265

A. K. Frailey Amazon Author Page

www.ingramcontent.com/pod-product-compliance
Lightning Source LLC
Chambersburg PA
CBHW070901180626
46817CB00003B/858